BOOKS BOOKS BOOKS
Issue nº 14 — Winter 2019

PART 1

On the cover, fashion designer GRACE WALES BONNER, photographed at the library by Alasdair McLellan.

PART 2

On the second cover, Joris-Karl Huysmans' 1884 masterpiece AGAINST NATURE, originally published in French as À REBOURS, a title also sometimes translated as AGAINST THE GRAIN.

Reproduction of an imitation: paper marbling
from the first edition of *À rebours*.

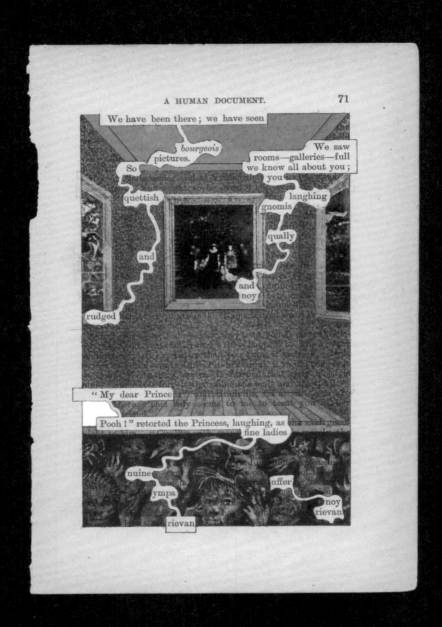

A HUMUMENT

In 1966, British artist TOM PHILLIPS bought a second-hand book with the intention of painting and collaging over every single page. The book was *A Human Document* by W.H. Mallock. In the spirit of alteration the title of his version dropped five letters to become *A Humument*, the first edition of which was printed in 1973.

RIPPED UP

It used to be so simple. Every book club was as follows: a group of friends met regularly to talk about a book they had just read. And that was it. What variables there were — where do we meet? How often? Who gets to be a member? How do we choose the next book? — posed no more of a logistical challenge than a night at the movies. In the purist book club, excitement and controversy could only emanate from a single source: the scrutinized text being squeezed through the personalities in the room.

Which was nice and worked well. But literary fetishes are more varied than the standard format could ever accommodate, and the world has filled with alternative set-ups, communal reading experiments offering adventure or exercise, philosophy societies and night-bus cabals to sate members' needs as they really are. Real-world examples include: a book club in which nobody reads the same book but rather each member presents a recent favourite; a WhatsApp-based book club whose members read ten pages of *Finnegans Wake* per day; a book club attended only by women, and in which nobody wears a top; a book club confined to biographies of football players; a book club dedicated to the romance novels of Jilly Cooper; and a book club during which members just sit together and read in silence.

One revolutionary configuration is the so-called invisible book club. This format was invented ten years ago by the writer and artist James Bridle. It is identical to the standard formula described above except in one respect, namely that while everybody reads the same book they are not allowed to talk about it. The images and ideas of which it consists rattle around the room. It is a kind of flirtation — or perhaps a sort of 'sphallolalia' — a too-rare word meaning 'flirtatious talk that goes nowhere'. It cuts to the part of the evening favoured by a significant minority, when the conversation moves onto general matters even while the world of the book remains in everybody's mind. It's forgiving, at least superficially, for those who didn't get round to reading the book at all.

The Happy Reader is a book club printed on paper. It's five years old this issue and has met fourteen times. It offers a communal read for all who want to join in. Forever recruiting readers, from Plymouth to Paris to La Paz, it wants to reach the entire planet, to turn the world into an invisible book club of sorts so that for six months at a time a book is just discreetly, nebulously floating in the air. One day, to test the water, you drop a jewel-encrusted tortoise into a conversation. The postman slyly nods. He knows exactly what you're talking about.

THE HAPPY READER
Bookish Magazine
Issue nº 14 — Winter 2019

The Happy Reader is a collaboration between Penguin Books and Fantastic Man

EDITOR-IN-CHIEF
Seb Emina

MANAGING EDITOR
Maria Bedford

ART DIRECTOR
Tom Etherington

EDITORIAL DIRECTORS
Jop van Bennekom
Gert Jonkers

PICTURE RESEARCH
Frances Roper

PRODUCTION
Ilaria Rovera

BRAND DIRECTOR
Sam Voulters

MARKETING DIRECTOR
Ingrid Matts

PUBLISHER
Stefan McGrath

CONTRIBUTORS
Jeremy Allen, Anuschka Blommers, Rene Burri, Tara Isabella Burton, Jarvis Cocker, Lydia Davis, Rob Doyle, Tony Frank, Richard Godwin, Gert Jonkers, Alasdair McLellan, Jamie MacRae, Nina Martyris, Andy Miller, Yelena Moskovich, Ben Okri, Tom Phillips, Niels Schumm.

THANK YOU
Magnus Åkesson, Ernst van der Hoeven, Matthew Hutchinson, Rebecca Lee, Penny Martin, Francisca Monteiro, Richard O'Mahony, Liz Parsons, Lindsey Tramuta, Antonia Webb.

DISTRIBUTED BY
boutiquemags.com

Penguin Books
80 Strand
London WC2R 0RL

info@thehappyreader.com
www.thehappyreader.com

SNIPPETS

North, east, west and south. Our essential survey
of the bookish and bound

YES
I WILL

BUT
HER
EMAILS

PREPPER

HUMBLE

Extinction Rebellion co-founder Gail Bradbrook has advice for those joining the climate protests: bring books. 'I never forget to carry a couple of good books,' she said, in an interview with *The Happy Reader*'s sister publication *The Gentlewoman*. 'If you happen to be arrested that day, you'll need something to do in the cell for eight hours.'

As the US presidential primaries enter their hairiest stages it's easy to forget a curious detail: three of the top Democrat contenders say James Joyce's *Ulysses* is one of their favourite books. Former Vice President Joe Biden has often namedropped the hard-to-finish classic. Veteran mayor Pete Buttigieg told *Bookriot* he thinks it's 'the greatest work of modern English literature'. Texan congressman Beto O'Rourke's son is literally called Ulysses. And back in Britain, Jeremy Corbyn is a fan too! 'Don't beat yourself up if you don't understand it,' the Labour leader has advised prospective readers.

Meanwhile, Hillary Clinton took a trip to this year's Venice Art Biennale and was surprised to find several bound copies of her leaked emails from 2016 lying on a replica of the Oval Office Desk. This was *HILLARY: The Hillary Clinton Emails*, an installation by American artist and poet Kenneth Goldsmith. 'This exhibition is proof that nothing wrong or controversial can be found on these emails,' she said, after sitting at the desk with them for about an hour. 'They are just a bunch of boring emails.'

During a game of cricket, Virat Kohli, the popular captain of the Indian national team, was spotted in the dressing room reading a self-help book called *Detox Your Ego*.

CLEVER

Words from old books keep leaking into corners of life where you wouldn't expect to find them: a sort of intellectual concrete. For example: Spoke, a clothes brand in London, makes trousers whose lining is covered in George Orwell's essay 'Politics and the English Language', and the Plaza de España metro station in Madrid recently removed all ads and printed the entirety of Miguel de Cervantes' novel *Don Quixote* on its walls instead.

'BOOK'

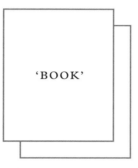

What is a book anyway? Certainly this question is forever in the air at Parisian studio Three Star Books, which is entirely dedicated to books devised by contemporary artists. There's a book that's an 'inventory of glitter' and a book made from a second-hand fur coat. There's a pile of books pierced by a kebab skewer. Most recently, there's a twenty-four page collaboration with Jonathan Monk in reference to the twenty-four frames in one second of a movie: an artist's version of the end credits of a film.

BRONX

When Barnes & Noble closed their Bronx branch in 2016, it left the New York borough more or less book-shop-free. The crisis was finally solved earlier this year when Bronx local Noëlle Santos opened the Lit Bar, an independent bookstore and wine bar. Drop by for books, tastings and events: 131 Alexander Ave, Mott Haven.

TRUE CRIME

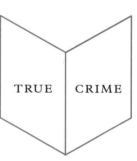

A student sleuth unmasked a prolific book thief, who has been jailed for twenty-five months. In the space of a year Darren Barr stole thousands of books from university campuses in Edinburgh that he would then resell online, trousering an estimated £30,000. He was caught when a PhD candidate bought a copy of a book from a website having been unable to find any of the six copies supposedly stocked by her university library. When it arrived she noticed it had in fact come from the library: a fake withdrawal notice had been added in an attempt to disguise the theft.

GRACE WALES BONNER

In conversation with
BEN OKRI

Portraits by
ALASDAIR McLELLAN

Grace Wales Bonner is a 28-year-old fashion designer from southeast London. The world of serious culture adores her (last year she curated a show at the Serpentine Gallery) as does the arena of glamour and celebrity (Meghan Markle wears Wales Bonner). But here's the unusual part: her clothes come with reading lists. In this conversation with Nigerian author and poet Ben Okri, she explains how essentially she sees herself as a researcher. She visits libraries, digests acres of complex ideas about politics and identity, and expresses them, among other things, via the realm of clothes. The covering of one's body doesn't get more seriously interesting.

LONDON

I first met Grace Wales Bonner in the offices of the Serpentine Gallery. Hans Ulrich Obrist, the magus of the gallery, had invited me to a mysterious meeting with Grace. They were in the planning stages for an exhibition. Hans had asked Grace who she would like to work with and she had mentioned my name. When I arrived I found myself sitting next to this beautiful, shy and silent young woman. She had an aura of calm and reserve. But when she spoke, her voice gentle, her ideas had clarity. She knew what she wanted. She asked how I would like to work with her and as I spoke I was struck by the depth of her listening. It immediately became clear that she was immensely well read, and that her reading was spread across the vistas of all the arts, from literature to fine art, music and dance and the obscure reaches of critical theory.

I'd heard about Grace Wales Bonner over the previous few years. She was a fashion designer who had been hailed as something of a wunderkind and polymath. Her collections are renowned for their edginess, their beauty and their originality. Among recent collectors of her work are figures like Meghan Markle.

We met many more times as the idea for the exhibition slowly became a reality. Collaborating with her that closely I got to see the mixture of her perfectionism and her intuitiveness at work. I experienced her generosity of vision and her love of collaboration. She insisted on all the different media of art having an equal status in the exhibition; so photography was presented like painting and poetry had the same status on the walls as a large canvas. When they were putting up one of my poems Grace had come in and seen how small it was on the wall. 'Make it bigger,' she said. Eventually they made it fill the size of the wall, giving the words a magnified impact. She did that with the music, the shrines, and made a special place for the African American poet and novelist Ishmael Reed. In all of this she seemed to put herself behind and everyone else in front. But she is not self-effacing, only profoundly respectful of the people she collaborates with. Perhaps she had long grasped the principle that you are only as good as the people you work with. But then again, perhaps she had grasped the greater principle that like attracts like, that magic draws magic.

The exhibition, staged in September 2018, was called *A Time for New Dreams*, and it broke new ground in the art of curating. It was a huge success, bringing in a diverse audience. The last day of the exhibition featured the launch of her new collection, to an audience including people like Naomi Campbell and Jools Holland. It was a new level in her meteoric rise. At a single stroke, Grace Wales Bonner was at the forefront of a new generation of designer artists.

She brings a holistic approach to design, and a fresh ethical perspective; she combines an intellectual and emotional dimension, informed by feminism, but honouring the masculine. Many traditions meet in her, including haute couture and the inspiration of the black diaspora. All of this is fused with a lightness of touch and a sense of humour.

Grace is a serious reader; the title of her exhibition came from the title of a volume of my essays. She also loves a good conversation. This one took place, at Grace's request, at the International Institute of Visual Art (INIVA), which houses the Stuart Hall library, in Pimlico.

There are few things that enrich a culture more than the art of conversation. Surrender yourself to this delicate and intuitive mind.

BEN: You know how many of our parents have this idea that we should choose one of the three dependable professions — engineering, law or medicine — and how that kind of structures the way in which we approach our future. Did you have any of that?

GRACE: My father was a lawyer, but my sense of career choices was quite open. I was open. I was encouraged in my interests. The creative and the academic were spaces I was nudged towards. But I think that this idea of reading and amassing a library and a thoughtful kind of contemplation was something I was aware of from my father. Just seeing him having quiet time to read and learning that collecting books was quite a sacred act was important for me. When I was growing up I was aware of that physicality and space. I feel like the idea of the black intellectual comes from that kind of study environment. I feel it as a mood as well.

B: We have a lot in common — our fathers are lawyers, books and reading had a sacred air. What is your earliest memory of the book as an object?

G: It came from my father, and it was seeing *Ulysses*.

B: What do you mean, seeing *Ulysses*?

G: The book.

B: Joyce's book?

G: Yeah. And he talked about Bloomsday.

B: Really?

G: It was on my sister's birthday.

Grace began her career specialising in fashion for men, adding womens-wear to her repertoire only in 2018.

B: June 16?

G: Yeah, exactly. We remembered Bloomsday because of that. He also liked Dylan Thomas's *Under Milk Wood*. I knew the title before the book.

B: I'm intrigued. How is it that you had this encouragement towards creativity? How come you were not pressurized towards a particular profession? It's a lucky thing to have had. Many of us had to fight against our parents' expectations.

G: I had an older sister who's quite academic. She went to Cambridge. So that was covered.

B: Yes, I can see that.

G: And I was always interested in history and identity. I access that through visual culture, through photography, images and self-reflection.

B: What's the earliest creative act you remember doing or witnessing?

G: Creative act?

B: Yes. My daughter, who's nearly three, knew me first as someone who draws, which is kind of weird. So she's taken over the whole drawing thing completely and I've left it to her. What was your earliest creative act?

G: I think it was movement. I did ballet and gymnastics when I was younger. I was quite in tune with my body; and elegant and graceful and precise about that.

B: You went to ballet school?

G: I went to ballet school and I did gymnastics as well.

B: You weren't tempted to become a dancer? You have a rich personal musical culture.

G: This is the special thing about my childhood. All avenues were kind of open. A lot of things were nurtured. Playing the piano, the violin, the trumpet...

B: So why did you choose the path you did?

G: I think I found a way to express myself most immediately.

B: In what?

G: In communicating, and probably in writing. I studied at Saint Martins. I was absorbing literature and theory, working on this dissertation about black rhythmicality. At the same time I was

1. DYLAN THOMAS
—
International Dylan Thomas Day is celebrated every year on the 14 May, the anniversary of the date on which *Under Milk Wood* – arguably Thomas's most famous work – was first read on stage in 1953 at 92Y The Poetry Center, New York.

2. SAINT MARTINS
—
Grace's peers in the class of 2014 included Kiko Kostadinov, a fellow nominee for the prestigious LVMH-prize, and cult British-Chinese-Vietnamese designer A Sai Ta.

3. ELIZABETH THE FIRST
—

An exhibition, 'The Lost Dress of Elizabeth I', currently on display at Hampton Court Palace displays a dress found in a church in the British countryside. It had been hidden in plain sight as the nice piece of cloth covering the altar.

working on my collection. In the end I realised that the clothing I'd made communicated all that I wanted to say, but in a much more immediate way. You didn't have to read what I was reading, but you could immediately see the depth and the nuances of what I was thinking about through the collection.

B: How did you get from this person who had all these avenues open to one who went in the direction of clothes, fabric, body movement, shapes? Did you make things when you were younger?

G: I think it was a gradual thing. But I was always drawing, collaging, working with imagery, contemplating and bringing things together. Collage was something I really enjoyed. I got into fashion very gradually. It was probably not until I was sixteen.

B: If someone had asked you 'what do you want to be?' around the age of ten, what would you have said?

G: I don't know. I didn't know what I wanted to be. Maybe a dancer, maybe a historian. I was very into history.

B: Interesting.

G: I was into Elizabeth the First.

B: Why?

G: I think because she was a strong, powerful, woman. I was interested in that. She stood out for that reason.

B: Not so much the period but more the woman?

G: I think the character. Then being an anomaly was quite interesting. I sometimes look out for those kind of characters.

B: You like anomalies, do you?

G: I like spaces where people can have the license to be something other than what they're supposed to be. I look for those opportunities. I look for those characters in history.

B: When we first met I was struck by your absorption in serious theoretical texts, by your interest in intellectual grounding. Do you read such texts for research or for pleasure?

G: I read them for pleasure. I read them to learn and to understand, which I find can be a larger thing. I went through a phase of not reading any fiction because the theoretical, historical texts were what I wanted to read, to get a sense of grounding.

B: I want to stay on childhood a little longer. Can you remember the earliest books you read as a kid? When I get asked that question I always have to move around the furniture of memory.

G: There was one book that I really loved called *Amazing Grace*. It's about a black girl who's an acrobat. She's about eight and she wears this spider costume. I think she's a dancer. The book's got really beautiful illustrations.

B: And it's for what age?

G: I must've been about eight.

B: You must have encountered books before eight. Fairytales and children's books. Did your mum read to you as a kid?

G: I remember Enid Blyton. And *Animal Farm*. Even when I really didn't understand it, my dad was reading *Animal Farm* to us.

B: How many of you were there in the family?

G: Three girls. I'm the middle.

B: Were you one of those children who is between cultures in your experience of books? Were you British in your reading?

G: As a child I was reading quite classical and British and American books. But it was when I was a teenager that I began discovering and identifying points of reference that felt more familiar. When I did find the opportunity to see something that reflected myself, like *Amazing Grace*, I would hold onto it.

B: Tell me about *Amazing Grace*. Have you still got it?

G: I haven't but I looked it up recently. There's a beautiful hardback. It had these lovely watercolour illustrations that were quite Caribbean and a smiling girl on the front cover.

B: It was identity in a way. From what you're saying that's your first sense of a book that reflected you, that doubled your presence in a way.

G: And I remember when I was twelve there was a book about these two mixed-race girls. One of them looked white and the other one was darker. It was about their different lives. They had completely different lives.

B: And they were friends?

G: They were sisters. The lighter one ended up living with her mum who then had this life on the road.

B: What happened to the darker one?

G: I think she had a strict education. But the other one's mum

4. HOMI BHABHA
—
Homi K. Bhabha is an important theorist in postcolonial theory, but his prose has sometimes been criticised for its density. In 1998 he won second prize in the *Philosophy and Literature* journal's 'Bad Writing Contest'. Responding to such criticism in a later interview he said, 'The idea that sources from the humanities have no philosophical language of their own, that they must be continually speaking in the common language of the common person while the scientists can publish in a language that needs more time to get into, is problematic to me.'

became a lesbian and was kind of on the road driving around. They were much more free. Much more hippy.

B: When I was a kid, I used to read late at night, under the covers, because of strict sleeping hours. I had a little torch. Would you say reading for you is conforming or transgressing?

G: I think it's like coming home to something I've felt but haven't seen articulated in words. I think it's about discovery. But discovering something I feel deep down, something that connects me to a different history, a different time, connects me to something that's more about feeling.

B: What was your dissertation about?

G: It was about representing rhythmicality through aesthetics in black artists like [Jean-Michel] Basquiat. It was thinking about him and Charlie Parker, about this way of representing space in a much more abstract mosaic kind of way, understanding space as opposed to something quite linear. It's about rhythms within aesthetics and how you could understand space in that way.

B: Why were you interested in such a complex subject? What drew you to want to explore that?

G: I've always been interested in rhythm, how it manifests and how it might inform ways of being or ways of creating. I remember reading an important book about black women's lives in Britain. It was a collection of autobiographical texts. One of the texts talks about how when the child's in the mother's womb, it feels the way the mother walks. The child gets its sense of rhythm through that. I found that interesting. Also from my travels I remember seeing how kids were moving and how it was such a natural part of being able to dance when you're two, just being so effortless and integrated. I think I was interested in how the body knows and remembers, how it has a memory.

B: What was the range of books you had to read for this thesis?

G: I was reading a book about drumming. A book called *Different Drummers*. It's about how drumming patterns have affected different cultures and different movements. There's one about drumming in the Haitian revolution. I read Homi Bhabha's *The Location of Culture*. That probably introduced me to Fred Martin and then Henry Gates and Greg Tate. I'm really interested in how rhythm informs different behavioural tropes and also in ways of speaking and ways of moving, ways of wearing clothes. When I think about the writers that I really love I think I've seen new ways of seeing. Writers describe something aesthetic also with rhythmical language. That's the kind of space I'm

Image: Mondadori Portfolio/Bridgeman Images

really interested in. Fred Martin's work is a really important grounding point for me but also 'The Field Trio'. I really love that poem. Also, I remember reading some poetry that you'd written for David Hammons in *Give Me a Moment*. I remember having that book and thinking about just how you absorb something aesthetic and articulate it in a really pure way. This pure rhythmic sense of communicating is also something I'm very interested in. It's the refining of form into something very direct.

B: You are a paradox. Your interests are intellectual but you've got so many sides that are so playful. Your work is playful and thoughtful. For example, you have a secret career as a DJ. Are these interests a continuation of that encouragement that you said you had as a kid, to follow all roads? Are you still doing that?

G: When I was graduating from Saint Martins I could have been a writer. I was building myself up to have something if things didn't work out. I was hedging my bets. That's why I extended what I was doing. But I then realised it's because of that extension that what I'm doing in fashion is interesting. That research background is interesting. It influences how I communicate. I need that stimulus to want to create. I wouldn't be able to create from the purely visual. It needs to be emotionally connected to my identity.

B: You had an exhibition at the Serpentine Gallery recently that was quite extraordinary. I was a part of it. Many people felt it broke new grounds in exhibition aesthetics. It was very different and fresh and new. When you work with fashion and bodies in fabric and research what is your philosophy? What are you constantly trying to do? Because I don't think it's one thing. I think it's a constantly evolving thing. Is it something that can be expressed, do you think?

G: I think initially what I was trying to do was broaden the spectrum of black representation within fashion and visual culture. I felt that I needed to be quite well committed but also repetitive in the sense of showing a myriad of ways of being and showing a spectrum of identity, which I didn't feel was being represented within fashion. That was my initial intention. I like to think of myself now as a researcher. Research grounds my creativity. But I have different ways of expressing ideas. One of them, the most direct, is fashion. Research can be a world or an environment. Research can be translated into literature, into music. I think at the core, it's about creating a world that is pieced together through fragments of literature, sound, images, histories. I'm really interested in collaboration and how people can connect to a central idea and expand it. Expand what the world is through their input as well.

B: I love collaboration. Most people are scared of it. Why are you so interested in collaboration?

G: I think I found it in 2015. I did a residency in northern Senegal for a month. It was in quite a rural area and I was researching textile traditions. But I was reading. Just reading, basically. And I had big plans about the work I'd be doing on that residency. I also worked on collages. In the end, I didn't create. I found a new way of working. I realised that to create I needed other people.

B: Isolation taught you that?

G: Yeah. After that, I was a lot more proactive about reaching out to people that I admired and opening up my research practice.

B: What happened? What was the light-bulb moment?

G: I think it was probably that I wasn't as productive as I had wanted to be. I had big plans about what I'd create, big expectations. But I was kind of isolated.

B: You said you did lots of reading. What did you take with you for that month? Did you take a whole truckload of books?

G: I had a lot of books. The main one I remember was *The Black Male* by Thelma Golden. It was the catalogue for one of her exhibitions. I remember there was a text by Greg Tate. I think it was about ten years after the exhibition and a lot of the issues felt exactly the same. I remember feeling shocked by that. I'm trying to think what else I was reading there. There were quite a lot of theoretical texts.

B: You like to accompany your exhibitions with books. Why is that? You've had about two or three of them, little booklets.

G: Yeah, little publications.

B: You have your own little publications which combines photographs and texts and poems.

G: It started when I created a series called *Everything is Real*. That was something I did for myself. It was a way of aggregating my research and looking at what informed a collection. I made the first one in maybe 2015 for my production, which was looking at *Reflections on Black Glove*. I remembered thinking about that and reading a lot of homoerotic literature. There was a really broad spectrum of influence in there. But what I really liked was when I was in Ghana... I was sixteen, maybe seventeen. It was a really important trip for me because I had gone on my own, or I'd gone with friends.

B: At sixteen?

G: I think I must've been seventeen. We went for a month. We wanted to travel all around but we went north. We went to Bolgatanga. And I remember everyone saying, 'Why are you going up there? That's pretty far.' People didn't often go there. But that was one of the most inspiring trips I've ever been on. It was very informative. I collected a lot of publications while I was there, small books that people were selling. They were these books for teenagers about love and relationships that were quite funny in the way they were written. The graphics were quite amazing. I was mixing these kinds of things I found in markets with very academic texts, with poetic texts of James Baldwin and just putting together these different references. It was exciting to use that formula for creating my own compositions. I remember I had Amiri Baraka's book, *In Our Terribleness*.

B: You showed it to me once.

G: I remember when I graduated from Saint Martins, I bought myself a signed copy. It was very expensive. It was about two hundred pounds, and it was a real commitment. That book was super inspiring in terms of the layout. The rhythmicality was expressed — his intonation was expressed — through the layouts as well. It also mixed graphics and photography. It was all a poem, but he saw the photographs by Billy Abernathy as a visual part in its own right. And it sounded right as well. I think that format was something that inspired *Everything is Real*, which is basically just documenting all the abstract things that come into that collection. I wanted to be methodical about the research, having a bibliography, recording and archiving the study. That's something I've continued to do with each collection. I highlight the references. I'm open about the inspiration.

B: Tell me about your first collection. What was it like to create that?

G: I'd just graduated. I must have been twenty.

B: How did you know that you could put together a collection?

G: Well, I'd done it as part of my graduate show, so I had to do that at the end.

B: What was the idea behind it?

G: I think I described it as looking at blaxploitation, a turning point in black expression, which was much more about taking complete ownership of your representation. Turning the camera on yourself and recording.

B: And holding the camera.

G: Holding the camera and the same with photography. Looking

5. BOLGATANGA
—
Ponds located near this northern Ghanian town are said to contain the friendliest crocodiles in Ghana, and perhaps the world.

6. JAMES BALDWIN
—
Despite living mostly in France in his later years, the American author kept an apartment in New York City. The building, which has this year been added to the National Register of Historic Places, is at 137 West 71st St.

Top: Edgar Arshakyan. Bottom: ADN-Bildarchiv/ullstein bild via Getty Images

at people as well. I was looking at a turning point in representation and also at a time where I thought in those images the men seemed very free and openly sensual and beautiful and elegant and sexy. But then thinking about where I was in 2014 it felt like we'd gone backwards in the way that men were expressing themselves or connected to an idea of beauty. I was thinking that there have been many examples in history where people have been more expressive and where the definition of masculinity has been broader. I was drawn to those examples, which is something I continued with my first official collection called *Ebonics*.

B: What does it mean?

G: Intonation, sound, how you pronounce something, rhythm. I was thinking about how you can know something is black through the rhythm, the sound. The sound of someone's voice. I was thinking about poetry, about someone like Amiri Baraka: when you see how something was written, you could feel how it was spoken as well. It was how you can kind of read blackness.

B: How did you translate that into your collection? Because you are talking here about ideas and literature and yet what you do is also very tactile, very visual.

G: My starting point is, you could say, literature. Then I'll think about visual references around the literature in order to create that world. I'll think about sounds that relate to that world and then I'll also think about textures that relate to that world, in terms of fabrication. But then I'll already have an idea of character through that research. I think I absorb a mood and I try to translate that mood into clothing.

B: That's quite something.

G: That's what I need to do. I need to have that kind of approach to want to create clothing. That's what inspires me.

B: Are your clothes meant to be read?

G: I've always thought about this idea of soulful or emotional dressing that's absorbing, the clothing being able to absorb a mood.

B: It also embodies narrative.

G: Yes, I also think about narrative in relation to a collection, how a character might evolve over a show.

B: What do you mean by a character in this instance?

G: I'll often be thinking of a specific character.

B: As inhabiting the clothes?

G: Yeah. And that character might evolve. So in one of my collections, *Blue Duets*, I was inspired by James Baldwin's writings and also Gary Fisher's notebooks. I was interested in this kind of hidden life. So I was thinking also about nightlife. There was a sequence where the characters were more 'day'. They had a utility job. Then they had this more transgressive side that was at night. Then they moved through the night and partied into the morning. You saw that evolution through the show.

B: So you have an invisible living character at the centre of that collection. The clothes are already peopled.

G: People inhabit the characters, in some ways. With my runway shows especially, I'll be casting people that can be that character and are believable in that character as well.

B: When we were talking once, at the Serpentine, you slightly resisted the idea of being called a fashion designer. How do you see yourself?

G: It depends. I see myself as a creative director. I have a creative vision for what it is that I'm creating and so I think it's a bit broader than a designer.

B: Is it because of all the other elements of research and mood?

G: I think so. I think of myself as an artist. I think of myself as a researcher. I also think of myself as a fashion designer. It depends. Sometimes I'll connect with different things but I do realise that fashion is the most immediate way for me to communicate.

B: I wanted to ask about your relationship to the times in which you find yourself. How do you research now, this time in which we live?

G: I think a lot about both history and now in terms of spirituality, not necessarily the news.

B: What are your spiritual texts? If there's such a thing for you.

G: At the moment I'm reading something about silence and meditation. I was also reading *Of Water and the Spirit*. Malidoma Patrice Somé. Through reading, I connect to now through spirituality.

B: Are you a slow reader or a fast reader?

G: Quite fast.

B: When you read, do you make a distinction between different media, like physical books or the internet?

G: I don't like to read on a screen.

7. MALIDOMA PATRICE SOMÉ
—
The Dagara people, into whom Malidoma Patrice Somé was born, believe that names are intrinsically linked to one's destiny. Malidoma roughly translates as 'friend of the stranger', and as such he was sent forward by the village elders to transport messages of ritual and indigenous wisdom to the West. Somé currently lives in Florida, and holds workshops, divinations and other rituals worldwide.

READ MY OUTFIT

Beyond the usual care instructions, Grace's clothes come with 'further reading'. After the interview she shared six key titles, each matched with the collection it influenced.

Images: courtesy Wales Bonner Studio

SPRING/SUMMER 2016
Collection: Malik
Book: *India in Africa, Africa in India* (2008)
Ed. John C. Hawley

—

Malik Ambar was born in Ethiopia in the sixteenth century, sold into slavery, then, eventually, freed in Western India, where he became Prime Minister of the Ahmadnagar Sultanate, a position of quite some power. 'Malik becomes a reflection on the unexpected,' say the official collection notes, 'an expression of the cross-cultural resonance that characterises the African diaspora across the Indian Ocean and further.' One inspiration was Hawley's edited collection of contributions from various disciplines — history, literature, sociology, dance — published by the Indiana University Press. (Extended reading lists for all Wales Bonner collections can be handily found at the label's official website, walesbonner.net)

SPRING/SUMMER 2018
Collection: Blue Duets
Book: *Gary in Your Pocket* (1996)
Gary Fisher

—

Gary Fisher was a black, gay writer born in 1961. Between studying English and creative writing at the University of North Carolina and his untimely death from AIDS at the age of just thirty-two, Fisher wrote extensively. He filled notebooks with drafts, poems and sketches, and documented quotidian life through countless journals and diaries filled with ticket stubs, clippings of sex ads taken from gay magazines and newspapers, Polaroid photographs and meticulously described thoughts, emotions and activities. Excerpts of these were published in 1996, two years after his passing, as *Gary in Your Pocket* by his friend — and future Brudner Prize winner — Eve Kosofsky Sedgwick.

AUTUMN/WINTER 2018
Collection: Des Hommes et Des Dieux
Book: *Notebook of a Return to the Native Land* (1939)
Aimé Césaire

—

Martinican poet and playwright Aimé Césaire was a radical intellectual and a founder of the 'négritude' movement, aiming to raise black consciousness in Africa and across the world. His epic poem *Notebook of a Return to the Native Land* was one of the movement's most notable works. Wales Bonner's collection draws on 'creole aesthetics, informed by French Caribbean philosophy' with other references including the plays and poems of Derek Walcott, the art criticism of Okwui Enwezor and the fiction of Marlon James.

SPRING/SUMMER 2019
Collection: Ecstatic Recital
Book: *Terry Adkins: Recital* (2017)
Ed. Ian Berry

—

Terry Roger Adkins is an interdisciplinary artist known for his sculpture, performance pieces, video installations and photography. Often inspired by or referencing specific musicians or instruments, Adkins referred to many of his exhibitions as 'recitals' — often presented alongside his collaborative performance group, the Lone Wolf Recital Corps. Wales Bonner's collection finds inspiration in the devotional rhythms of Adkins' works. The garments — like Adkins' found objects and sculptural instruments — are imbued with 'celestial vibrations', both literally and figuratively; buttons are replaced by tingsha bells, cufflinks by rose quartz, and all radiate spiritual energy in abundance.

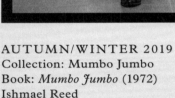

AUTUMN/WINTER 2019
Collection: Mumbo Jumbo
Book: *Mumbo Jumbo* (1972)
Ishmael Reed

—

Mumbo Jumbo centres around PaPa LaBas, a Harlem-based *houngan* or voodoo priest, and his efforts to take down the so called Wallflower Order — a monotheistic conspiracy dedicated, in essence, to the eradication of black freedom and artistic expression. It was written by poet, publisher and writer Ishmael Reed, a close collaborator of Grace's who played a jazz composition at the collection's presentation. The characters of the show mirror those within Reed's novel — mixing staple American collegiate garments such as the button-down shirt or the gabardine mackintosh with voodoo's talismanic totems. The result: varsity dress infused with 'an atavistic magic', weaving a 'sacred thread' between the 'intellectual brotherhood' of early 1980s Howard University (a historically black US college) and 'the animist traditions of West Africa and the Caribbean.'

SPRING/SUMMER 2020
Collection: Mambo
Book: *Aesthetic of the Cool* (2011)
Robert Farris Thompson

—

Robert Farris Thompson is one of America's foremost scholars of the Afro-Atlantic artistic world, in all its forms, but none more than mambo. Mambo, as a musical genre, might be widely acknowledged as being born in Cuba, but it has deep roots in west Africa. Thompson posits that Yoruba slaves taken from their homes and supplanted in northeastern Brazil and Cuba supplied the necessary multi-metric rhythms for the art form to thrive, spreading north and south throughout the Americas. In the third collection of a triptych dedicated to black spirituality, Wales Bonner looks to the 1940s — the years in which mambo was popularised — in terms of shape and silhouette, but retains the familiar motifs of Black Atlantic religion. Voodoo-inflected designs inspired by Haitian painter Hector Hyppolite sit on contemporary fabrications to allow, and demand, movement — hypnotic, rhythmic, devotional movement.

B: Oh, why not? I would have thought, being someone who does the amount of research that you do, you'd unavoidably be doing a lot of screen reading.

G: No. I like to either read physical books or scan things in the library and then highlight things. I don't like reading on a screen.

B: Why is that?

G: Because I spend too much time on the computer, so I don't find it relaxing.

B: And when you write?

G: I like to write in a notepad or on paper. I don't often translate that into a computer. When I'm writing on the computer, it's more practical.

B: What about writers of your generation, writers of now? Do you read books as a way of getting the inflections on what's going on? I know you like people like Zadie Smith and Toni Morrison. Do you read your generation, do you feel it necessary to do that? Or are you much more comfortable reading historically?

G: There's a certain lineage or form that I'm interested in, which could be from now or it could be from twenty years ago.

B: It was striking that you had a figure like Ishmael Reed at the Serpentine exhibition. He's kind of a legend in African-American literature. Wouldn't be very well known here. I was surprised that you had made that connection with his work, with that gap of time between you. You made a really living connection. How does that work? Do you just go by the gut feeling? I'm just struck by your crossing of time.

G: I'll read things and then it might be one or two years or five years later, where that becomes very relevant and necessary. Often I'm recalling something that I've read, and I'll have a vague idea or an emotional idea of what it is, an emotional idea of the characters. This will actually inform me. So it's a fragment of something, a memory of something that's made me feel a certain way that becomes important. That's why I'm broad in what I read. With Ishmael Reed, I was thinking about the idea of the writer as oracle. Writers having a very important role in connecting us to origin or to ancestry and also to Africa. And so I'm thinking about this lineage and I'm thinking about these threads that are created through thoughts and stories, thinking about the people that have made those connections. He's made very important connections in terms of the evolution of black thought. This idea of the black intellectual is something that he really embodies.

B: What does spirituality mean to you?

G: For me, it's a connection with the eternal.

B: The eternal in us or the eternal in which we are? Or both?

G: It'd be both.

B: Where did that sense come from, this sense of the spiritual?

G: I think it's through feeling.

B: What do you mean?

G: Through feeling as opposed to thinking. It's something I feel. In terms of ancestry and lineage, it was something I really was physically connecting to.

B: And by ancestry, you mean cultural ancestry? Is that also intellectual ancestry?

G: I think cultural. Really feeling a connection to my ancestors.

B: Both sides of your ancestry, you're talking about here?

G: I think it was more connecting to Africa. African ancestors and something abstract, but something that I really physically feel. It's hard to explain.

B: Something at your show that really moved people was having Laraaji do sound meditations. It was amazing. People were deeply touched and lifted by the spiritual possibilities of sound.

G: Laraaji is someone that really connects with the aesthetics of spirituality. And I was thinking about the form of a shrine as a portal. Sound can be a shrine. Sound can be a portal into another space.

B: Some people think of books as portals. And not just in the reading of them.

G: Really?

B: I remember shrines growing up in Nigeria, where you'll see an altar on which would be a stone and bunched feathers, and then there'll be a book. What was important was not the title or the author of the book, but its symbolic, liminal presence.

G: I remember in *The Famished Road* this idea of portals and emerging into another place, through the market. So I had these ideas of portals and going into different spaces or realms through your writing as well and also through Ishmael Reed's writing: *Mumbo Jumbo* and this collage of references and rhythm that goes in depth into another space. My understanding of spirituality and magical potential

8. LARAAJI
—
After being discovered by Brian Eno in 1979, playing zither in Washington Square Park, Laraaji has since become fundamental to the canon of New Age music; mixing vocal hymnals, chants and drones with electronically altered autoharps to create shimmering worshipful soundscapes. More recently he has become a frequent collaborator of Grace's. He has performed at her shows, been part of her 2019 Serpentine exhibition, and is a constant presence at her performance project Devotional Sound.

also came through those books. I wanted to honour that connection, so that was part of the shrine that I created as well.

B: You had lots of shrines in that show. You had books as shrines. You had televisions as shrines. Photographs. Do you still paint as an artist? Do you still make stuff? Do you now do collage?

G: I do collage. I don't do as much as I would like to. I think I'll come back to collage and writing.

B: Why do you think that your collections have caught people's imagination? People love your work. They love your collections and your clothes.

G: I think at first, I was surprised that people were willing to engage with or respond to what I was doing because it felt, initially, so personal. But I hope that they can see the emotion in what I'm doing.

B: Do your parents wear your clothes? You haven't made me the clothes you promised. You still owe me something.

G: I do.

B: She says wearily.

G: No, I do, I do.

B: Now I'm looking forward to it. Did you know my daughter wears your t-shirt? I got something for her from your collection.

G: Oh, amazing. We need to get you some robes.

B: Robes?

G: Yeah. My parents don't wear my clothes at the moment. Haven't got onto it yet.

B: That will come.

G: I remember reading something that you wrote, I think it was in *A Time for New Dreams*, about people's libraries. You said that it was important to have a library that has writers from all over the world. I remember liking that.

B: Thanks. That's because I've been to many people's houses. They invite you, you visit them, and you are just idly looking at their shelves, looking at their books. Then after a while you begin to notice the homogeneity of the books on their shelves. This is true of almost everybody I visited. There would be the standard hardback editions of Hardy, Dickens and Jane Austen. After a while, you think, 'What, no Toni Morrison, Chinua Achebe, James Baldwin, Pessoa, Márquez,

9. CHINUA ACHEBE
—
The celebrated Nigerian author, who died in 2013, shared Grace's fondness for writing with pen and paper. 'For one thing, I don't like to see mistakes on the typewriter,' he told the *Paris Review* in 1994. 'I will sometimes leave a phrase that is not right, not what I want, simply because to change it would be a bit messy.'

Taking a book out. Photo-
graphic assistance: Simon
Mackinlay, Peter Smith.
Make up: Lauren Parsons.
Hair: Ryan Mitchell.
Production: Jordan Kelly.

Petero Kalulé's poem 'Brilliant corners' is reproduced with thanks to Guillemot Press.

Borges, R.K. Narayan, Susan Sontag?' Then I find myself wondering how they could embrace the idea of humanity and be comfortable with people if they can't embrace them in books first. I think people's prejudices are reflected in the books on their bookshelves. This is because reading is one of the most intimate things we do. Making love is intimate. But with reading, you're letting someone right into your soul.

G: I was recently reading *A Way of Being Free* as well. You write about the magic of writing, and how people have to create in their minds. It is deeply, intimately connected to us.

B: What are you reading now? What are you carrying around? What do you carry around?
G: I'm reading this, actually. It's poetry.

B: Do you want to read me out a line? Read out a couple of lines? Who is it? Just tell us who it is.
G: Petero Kalulé.

B: And where is it from?
G: I'm not sure where it's from.

B: Where did you find this book?
G: At the South London Gallery.

B: And the book is called, let's just get the title.
G: *Kalimba*.

B: *Kalimba*.
G: 'Brilliant corners'.

> when
>   Monk & Sonny play,
> beatitudes of   syntax *s* wing fractal
>
> & beckon   lines of
>   circle & voice,   out
>   of   the   sentient
>   blue
>
> when
>   Monk & Roach & Sonny
>   fray
>   pitch awake,

31

brilliant orion spheres plectra
arabesque,

miming the black revenant amen of
susurrus shadow

B: I can see it's kind of fractal.

G: It's the idea of things that evoke a rhythm and evoke a picture through that as well.

B: You want to tell me about your DJ-ing and your whole music collage aspect?

G: Devotional Sound?

B: Yes. You take your DJ-ing quite seriously.

G: I see music as a kind of a research process as well.

B: What do you mean? What are you researching? Soundscapes?

G: Music within specific themes and moods. But I think I'm trying to approach my music sourcing in a similar way to the library. In the sense that what I'm interested in is very broad. I'm interested in music from all over the world, really.

B: You're also interested in film, aren't you?

G: I've made a few films in the past with Harley Weir and I think eventually film's something I'd like to be more involved with. I think it's synthesizing a mood. It's kind of the best format for that.

B: Apart from what you do, what do you think is the most expressive form of our age? Do you think film is more immediate, do you think music? What do you think catches this age?

G: Expressive in what way? Because I might think of dance as being more personally expressive, more intimate and intuitive.

10. CAPSULE
—

The two *Voyager* satellites, which are the only artificial objects to have left the Solar System, each carry a 'golden record' containing a variety of natural sounds (thunder, birds, whales) plus musical snippets and spoken greetings from a range of human cultures and eras.

B: If you wanted to send a capsule to some person on some far away planet and say, this will give you some sort of feeling of what it's like to be human right now, what would you send? Would you send bits of fabric? Would you send soundscapes? Would you send images? What captures the elusive essence of this time that we're breathing, that's passing, that someone will be researching in twenty years' time?

G: It's difficult. I'd probably have an urge to romanticize the part of time that is happening.

B: What would you romanticize?

Image: NASA/JPL

G: Probably a tenderness between people.

B: Are you quite political as well in a way? Do you have an activist side to you? Or a quiet activist side to you?

G: My politics are kind of embedded in how I express myself, but the way I express myself is very subtle, so it will be in keeping with that way of expressing myself.

B: So your politics are embedded in your aesthetics.

G: I think so. What are you reading at the moment?

B: What am I reading? Behind the right-wing groups of our time, behind Salvini and Trump and Farage, there are certain ideas which are coming back from an earlier incarnation in which things were done and turned out really badly. I'm talking about the '30s and the '40s. There were certain philosophers that gave intellectual structure to a lot of the stuff that was happening then. The fascist movements had their dubious intellectual foundations. They had their philosophers. Those same philosophers are being brought back and are being used by people like Steve Bannon to drive the new right-wing movements of the world. I'm researching that.

G: Wow.

B: I think it's important to understand the ideas behind those who are trying to change our world right now in negative ways.

G: Do you find it hard to handle the darkness of the present? I mean, creatively?

B: I'm comfortable handling darkness creatively. I always have been. I think it's because of my childhood in the [Nigerian] Civil War. I've always assumed that the darker element tends to be stronger in humanity. Look at history. It tends to be a record of the darker aspects, alongside resistance and creativity. That's why those on the side of light need to fight harder, with more will, more love, more courage, more creativity. Are you comfortable with handling darkness?

G: Let me think.

B: Can you stare at it? Do you like staring at it?

G: I can. But I think I'm really seeking out beauty, which I know is connected to darkness. I think I'm quite sensitive, so it's quite hard to absorb too much.

B: Yes. Me too. It took me a long time to toughen my spirit. It took a long time. I don't know if you've read *The Freedom Artist* yet?

G: I haven't read it yet, unfortunately.

B: In that book I deal with the dark undercurrents of now. I found the best way to do it was indirectly.

G: Yes.

B: So you see beauty as dealing with the dark side, with the darkness.

G: Not necessarily to deal with it, but it's what I'm drawn to. I'm drawn to expressing and revealing and I see that beauty is tinged with suffering as well.

B: What do you think we need right now? People feel lost, people feel powerless. The ones who don't feel powerless feel like they've tried and they didn't have any effect. Do you think we need to be soothed? Do you think we need to be shaken?

G: I think we need beauty. I think we need silence. And compassion. Compassion for ourselves, compassion for others.

B: Yes, but what do you do when the ones who have power don't have compassion for those who need it? What do you do when power just doesn't care and just imposes its agendas on us?

G: I find that I try and distance myself from that reality and try to find space in other places.

B: Can fashion help change the world?

G: I think influencing, in a subtle way, can have an important cultural impact.

B: Things you do have a visual and aesthetic impact on a lot of people. Do you think the artist has a valuable cultural or political role?

G: I think it's important to be prolific and committed and almost repetitive in your intention. I think that does have an impact on culture. There are artists and writers and designers who have created that space and hold their intention. I think that has reverberations.

B: So you're basically an optimistic artist?

G: I'd say so.

BEN OKRI is a poet, novelist and playwright. His novel, *The Famished Road*, won the Booker Prize in 1991. His latest novel is *The Freedom Artist*. His latest book, a volume of stories, is *Prayer for the Living*. He is being fitted for a Grace Wales Bonner suit.

THE HAPPY
READER

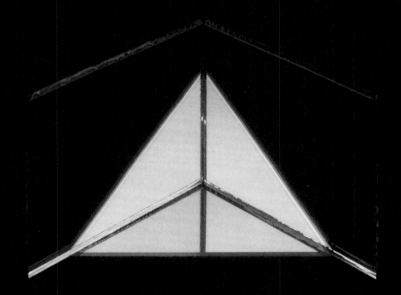

Joris-Karl Huysmans' ridiculously exquisite and bizarro 1884 tale AGAINST NATURE in 41 artefacts, 7 stories and 6 real nightmares.

"He scoured the suburbs of Paris and eventually discovered a villa for sale on the hillside above Fontenay-aux-Roses, standing in a lonely spot close to the Fort and far from all neighbours. This was the answer to his dreams, for in this district which had so far remained unspoilt by rampaging Parisians, he would be safe from molestation: the wretched state of communications, barely maintained by a comical railway at the far end of the town and a few little trams which came and went as they please, reassured him on this point."

ADDRESS
Two sentences from *Against Nature*'s prologue set the scene for a book confined to the inside of a house. Huysmans himself once lived in Fontenay-aux-Roses, probably at what is now 10 rue Boris Vildé.

INTRODUCTION

As we go about our seasonal accumulation of books, ornaments and other artefacts, one novel has the power to make us stop and wonder: what is all this stuff actually for? The relentless inventorying of *Against Nature* thrills and inspires some readers, baffles others, and as for ANDY MILLER he loves it mostly because it makes him laugh.

THE STRANGEST BOOK I'VE EVER READ

Last year a friend of mine read *Against Nature* by Joris-Karl Huysmans for the first time. They were not impressed. 'Anyone who claims this is one of their favourite books is absolutely bullshitting,' they told me. 'It's one of mine,' I said. A long silence followed.

There probably isn't a book I like thinking about more than *Against Nature*, more than I like reading it, in fact. It is a book to have finished, put back on the shelf or returned to the library. Then one can begin to enjoy it. Actually there probably isn't a book I like telling people I like thinking about more than *Against Nature* either. And look, I am doing all these things right now. QED, suckers!

I am not alone in either my enthusiasm or ambivalence. In a note to his translation of the novel, first published in 1957, Robert Baldick writes: 'Huysmans' style, which [Léon] Bloy described as "continually dragging Mother Image by the hair or the feet down the worm-eaten staircase of terrified Syntax", is one of the strangest literary idioms in existence, packed with purple passages, intricate sentences, weird metaphors, unexpected tense changes and a vocabulary rich in slang and technical terms ... it is only fair to warn the reader that he may find that the resultant mixture,

like the French original, is best taken in small doses.'

And yet, *Against Nature* really is one of my favourite books; and if I am bullshitting, I am not bullshitting absolutely or at least no more than anyone who loves a book when an element of the book's appeal is the notion of it becoming a personal favourite and of being able — truthfully, delightedly — to claim it. Most books are like other books, except *Against Nature* and a handful of others: *The Ragged-Trousered Philanthropists*, *By Grand Central Station I Sat Down and Wept*, *The Moon's a Balloon*. But equally, mind how you go.

Against Nature is composed of three unstable elements: decadence, boredom and hilarity. Any one of these ingredients by itself would present a risk but combining them is potentially lethal. Depending on the reader, J.-K. Huysmans is either a parfumier or a bomb-maker; allow me to fetch the tongs and let's see what we're dealing with.

Against Nature's claim to literary significance is in Arthur Symons' famous image, as a 'breviary' of decadence. 'Elaborately and deliberately perverse,' wrote the English critic in 1893, 'it is in its very perversity that Huysmans' work — so fascinating, so repellent,

so instinctively artificial — comes to represent, as the work of no other writer can be said to do, the main tendencies, the chief results, of the Decadent movement in literature'.

On publication in May 1884, this account of a sickly young aristocrat who retreats to an isolated villa where he indulges his appetite for luxury and excess caused a sensation. Sixty years after it first appeared in an English translation, the book continues to be a document of historical importance to generations of British school children, who learn about it via Oscar Wilde's *The Picture of Dorian Gray*: it is generally agreed to be the 'poisonous French novel' that drives the main character to self-destruct. The synopsis in Wilde's novel is elegant:

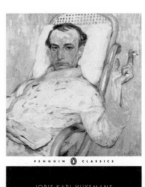

MULBERRY
*Gives a juice like
soot-stained wine.*
CAT. Food & Beverage

'It was the strangest book that he had ever read. It seemed to him that in exquisite raiment, and to the delicate sound of flutes, the sins of the world were passing in dumb show before him ... It was a novel without a plot, and with only one character, being, indeed, simply a psychological study of a certain young Parisian, who spent his life trying to realize in the nineteenth century all the passions and modes of thought that belonged to every century except his own.'

Against Nature is decadent in both style and substance. It isn't simply that the novel is a repository of the trappings of the Decadence — exquisite perfumes, furniture, foods and fashions — and the Decadents' attitudes to contemporary philosophy, politics and religion. It is also decadent in how it torments the reader with a slow-moving parade of the aforementioned purple passages, intricate sentences and weird metaphors. Despite what Dorian Gray may believe, the novel does have a wisp of a plot: jaded aesthete secludes himself in provinces, unsuccessfully. It almost entirely lacks drama, however, and when drama

PLUM PUDDING
*Pairing suggestions:
Valdepeñas, Oporto.*
CAT. Food & Beverage

is manifested, its purpose is principally to dramatise the author's disdain for dramatic convention. The jewel-encrusted tortoise crawls its way across the room but never arrives.

Which brings us to boredom. In *Against Nature*, Huysmans treats tedium as though it were drama — and the tension never lets up. Symons' comparison of the book to a breviary is useful here. A breviary is another kind of book 'without a plot', an assortment of psalms, hymns and selected parts of Holy Scriptures read daily by ordained clergymen of the Roman Catholic Church, the purpose of which is liturgical and the effect mesmerising, exactly like the 'poisonous novel' described by Dorian Gray: 'The mere cadence of the sentences, the subtle monotony of their music, so full as it was of complex refrains and movements elaborately repeated, produced

OLIVE
From Turkey.
CAT. Food & Beverage

in the mind of the lad, as he passed from chapter to chapter, a form of reverie...'

As Huysmans intones the repetitious inventory of books, scents, pictures, opinions, gripes and ailments, we can respond in one of three ways. The reader may feel like Des Esseintes in Chapter 5, contemplating Odilon Redon's drawings: 'His gloom would then be dissipated, as if by magic; a sweet sadness, an almost languorous sorrow would gently take possession of his thoughts, and he would meditate for hours in front of this work.'

Another legitimate response to *Against Nature*'s drone of decadent plainsong might be to put the book down and read something else instead. But a third response — and one not mutually exclusive to the first two — is laughter.

RYE BREAD
While a hidden orchestra plays.
CAT. Food & Beverage

Bruce Robinson, the writer and director of the cult British film *Withnail & I*, has described *Against Nature* as 'the funniest book ever written'; Marwood (AKA 'I') has a copy of the book in his suitcase at the end of the film and one can detect Des Esseintes in Withnail's decadent appetites and pharmacological expertise, not to mention the richness of his vocabulary. The protagonists of both book and film flee the city in order to 'get into the countryside, rejuvenate' and 'take refuge from the incessant deluge of human stupidity'. But what Robinson really seems to have responded to is the spleen bubbling constantly just beneath the surface of the novel, which erupts in fiery denunciations of this writer or that painter; that and the bit with the tortoise. (I once saw Robinson incapacitated with laughter as he tried to explain the latter scene to an interviewer.)

For me, the book's air of decadence and tedium creates an atmosphere in which Des Esseintes' various doomed attempts to alleviate his ennui become, through repetition and absurdity, more and more hilarious. Chapter 11 of *Against*

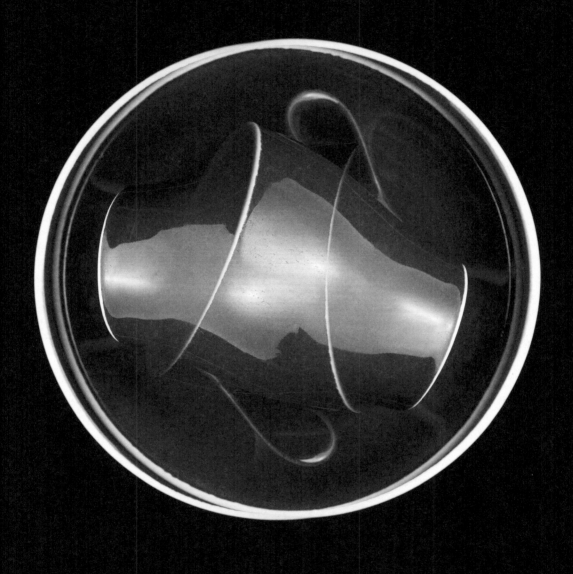

ILLUSION
'At five o'clock in winter, after dusk had fallen, he ate a light breakfast of two boiled eggs, toast and tea; then he had lunch about eleven, drank coffee or sometimes tea and wine during the night and finally toyed with a little supper about five in the morning, before going to bed.' (Image here and on pages 35, 47, and 55 by BLOMMERS/SCHUMM)

Nature, in which Des Esseintes decides to sail to England but gets no further than a tavern near the Gare Saint-Lazare, may be the funniest thing ever written. 'I've been steeped in English life since I left home, and it would be madness to risk spoiling such unforgettable experiences by a clumsy change of locality,' muses our hero near the end of his aborted adventure, a sentiment which finds its modern analogue in Homer Simpson's 'What's the point of going out? We're just gonna wind up back here anyway'.

What underpins *Against Nature*, as it often underpins a joke we find funny, is truth. So adept was Huysmans at depicting a soul in torment, defeated repeatedly by an indifferent universe of his own making, he created an archetype; that he did so without recourse to much in the way of plot, structure or pleasing syntax is all the more endearing. Furthermore, each generation sees itself reflected in *Against Nature*; decadence for the late Victorians, 'opting out' for the 1960s counterculture, and for those living through

late capitalism, a portrait of the individual with a surfeit of everything. It is both the least relatable book of all time and the most.

If you only read one book this year, make sure it's worth it. I recommend *Against Nature*.

ANDY MILLER is a reader, author and editor of books, and co-host of the literary podcast *Backlisted*. He first read and fell in love with *Against Nature* in 2006 when preparing to write his literary memoir *The Year of Reading Dangerously*; he describes his contribution to this issue as 'the chapter that never was'.

NIGHTMARE
by Jarvis Cocker

I was viewing a run-down country house with massive grounds. The proportions were all wrong and there was a lot of traffic noise due to a nearby overpass. In the forest were giant woodlice about as big as a human fist. There was a song you could sing that could destroy the infestation. It could either be sung by a lone polecat or a children's choir. An albino polecat had apparently killed all the insects on a country lane. We recorded a choral version in a church. During the playback one of the kids was messing with the church organ and put a bass line under the track. Their teacher told her off but I thought it sounded good. I found a bass and asked to do an overdub. There was no click-track. The bass got caught under a door making it very hard to reach the fretboard. Somehow I played along (it was on the 3rd string — 5th fret x1, open x1, 5th fret x2, open x1).

INTERIORS

The extravagant twentieth-century polymath Serge Gainsbourg loved *Against Nature* — in fact it was the blueprint for his home. JEREMY ALLEN tours a relic of glorious artifice, an eccentric and landlocked *Mary Celeste*.

CHEZ GAINSBOURG

There's an apartment on Paris's left bank a few hundred metres from the River Seine that is of great French national interest, though nobody has lived there for nearly three decades. 5 bis rue de Verneuil, situated where the plush 6th arrondissement meets the touristy 7th, is where Serge Gainsbourg resided from the late sixties until his death

in 1991. The graffiti on the wall outside, daubed extravagantly on an otherwise bourgeois street, evolves according to the whims of his fans, but the interior hasn't changed since pompiers had to break in on a March morning to recover the French singer's body.

Gainsbourg was born in Paris in 1928 to Russian Jewish

refugees. He was known to the British for many years as a one-hit wonder, for the steamy 1969 single 'Je t'aime... moi non plus', recorded with virginal choirboy singing and sexual simulation from Jane Birkin, nineteen years old at the time and nineteen years Gainsbourg's junior. The fact it was too hot for the Vatican and the

BBC didn't stop it selling six million copies.

Although Gainsbourg's name was mentioned rarely in Britain outside of pub quizzes while he was still alive, in the '90s something strange happened. His work was sampled by hip-hop artists and his album *Histoire de Melody Nelson* stealthily became part of the classic rock canon, while his name became a cool one

CHRYSOBERYL
A strong asparagus green.
CAT. Home

to drop. Further excavation revealed a renaissance man and polymath with an extraordinary and eclectic back catalogue with chansons about sex (naturally), incest, pederasty, Nazis, shit, alcoholism and death. Sacha Distel he wasn't.

His apartment too is atypical — a dark sarcophagus festooned with bizarre treasures and eccentric keepsakes, a cabinet of curiosities that's the very embodiment of the dandy provocateur's strange tastes. If that sounds like something out of the pages of J.-K. Huysmans, then it's entirely intentional. 'It is quite clear that the interior of the Rue de Verneuil house-museum, designed by Serge Gainsbourg with a maniacal passion, is like one of Des Esseintes' dreams,' wrote Bertrand Dicale in his 2009 biography *Gainsbourg en dix leçons*. 'Surgical tools, police badges, precious boxes, a tarantula ... it's a snob's junkyard of arbitrary delights.'

'Serge Gainsbourg owned an original edition of *Against Nature* with the pages worn from being read and re-read so

much,' concurred the art critic Franck Maubert (in a book called *Gainsbourg À rebours*). 'It was his bible, his blueprint and his secret reference. He could recite passages by heart to anyone who would care to listen.' When Gainsbourg opened his doors to Maubert for an interview in 1986, he too was struck by the Huysmanian nature of the apartment, its dining table decorated with a black table cloth, violets and purple wildflowers. 'I had the uncomfortable sensation of entering a coffin,' he wrote, 'an impression quickly belied by the rather joyous mood of the master of the house, though he was also tinged with a certain melancholy.'

Gainsbourg was seemingly so in thrall to Huysmans' *roman à clef* that he assumed the narrator's contradictory state of mind as well as his design foibles. A first impression of the apartment's interior suggests disorder but in fact each object is arranged meticulously to the point of derangement. Des Esseintes' vials and jars 'piled on top of each other in utter confusion' could be a

SAPPHIRINE
Bluish, phosphorescent fire against a dull, chocolate brown background.
CAT. Home

description of chez Gainsbourg, while the protagonist's distress at his books 'stacked higgledy-piggledy on their shelves' could equally refer to the singer's compulsiveness, according to the people who knew him best.

'Everything is the way he wanted it,' says his daughter Charlotte Gainsbourg, the sole proprietor of 5 bis after she bought out the shares belonging to Serge's three other children soon after his death. 'There are tonnes of objects that had not only a specific spot, but also orientation, and it would mean you would have to put the lady figurine or the little man in exactly the right spot or my father would notice.'

Serge Gainsbourg bought the property outright in 1968 with the money he made from

PERIDOT
A definite leek green
CAT. Home

WORLD OF INTERIORS
A photograph by TONY FRANK of Serge Gainsbourg's apartment in Paris, untouched and barely visited since the singer died in 1991.

UVAROVITE
*Flashes with harsh,
brilliant light.*
CAT. Home

Yé-yé ingénue France Gall's 'Poupée de cire, poupée de son', an international hit that won the Eurovision Song Contest for Luxembourg in 1965. Soon after the acquisition he met the English actress Jane Birkin, who would give birth to Charlotte, their only daughter, in 1971. While they lived there for eleven mostly happy years, Birkin felt imprisoned by the fussiness at times. 'He was a maniac,' she told me. 'For me it was a nightmare to live in Rue de Verneuil. It was exquisite to be able to give him presents because he used to put them in a place and he'd say, "From now on, nobody will touch it." And so I used to buy him bronzed rats from Japan or medical things he'd put on his table, or tapestries for the wall. But it was a museum.'

BALAS RUBY
*Vinegar-pink with
a feeble lustre.*
CAT. Home

So what of the contents? The apartment is inspired by, rather than an outright imitation of, Des Esseintes' country hideaway. A faithful recreation would have contravened the dandy code, which values originality above all else. What's more, to track down those Gustave Moreau paintings and Jan Luyken engravings would have been unfeasible. So instead of an ivory astrolabe — a multi-purpose astronomical sphere that was popular in medieval times — you'll find an aspherical nineteenth-century patinated bronze pumpkin in the bar, surrounding a far more functional engraved glass liquor decanter. There's ebony wooden paneling in the salon, like in Des Esseintes' place, but it's in the Art Deco style that postdates *Against Nature*. Instead of a bejewelled and gold-painted dead tortoise in

ALAMANDINE
Like the insides of wine casks.
CAT. Home

the boudoir there's a nineteenth-century globe-mounted tarantula on brass wire by the Maison Deyrolle, specialists in taxidermy and pedagogical charts. What's more, Gainsbourg's books in his study hark back to the French decadence, while Des Esseintes' collection of Latin tomes are more concerned with the classical decadence.

There's a triptych of framed Baudelaire sonnets on vellum parchment in *Against Nature*; Gainsbourg instead acquired a scroll of 'La Marseillaise' handwritten by the author Claude Joseph Rouget de Lisle himself. Gainsbourg sang lyrics from the French national anthem on his hit 1979 song 'Aux armes et cætera' recorded with some celebrated Jamaican reggae musicians; it caused a scandal and provoked a number of antisemitic attacks in the press and the threat of a

TURQUOISE
*Simply a fossil ivory impregnated
with coppery substances.*
CAT. Home

lynching by paramilitaries at a gig in Strasbourg. To have such a document of patriotic pride in his possession would have been a thumb in the eye to his racist detractors.

Other artworks that adorn Rue de Verneuil also informed his work: Paul Klee's 1913 sketch *Mauvaises nouvelles des étoiles* became the name of his second reggae album in 1981, a subpar follow-up with a track that merely features the sound of breaking wind over ska backing, and Claude Lalanne's cabbage-head sculpture *L'Homme à tête de chou*, which became a 1976 concept album about a man living in a hotel who beats his partner to death with a fire extinguisher.

To be fair, the influence of Huysmans was occasionally augmented by other larger-than-life figures from art's recent history. Some of Salvador Dalí's interior choices informed those of Rue de Verneuil, and the story of why is worth recounting. Gainsbourg's first wife Elizabeth 'Lize' Levitsky was working in the office of the Dadaist artist George Hugnet in the late '40s and somehow laid her hands

CEYLON'S CAT'S EYES
*Greenish grey streaked
with concentric veins.*
CAT. Home

on the house keys of the Father of Surrealism. Lize and Serge audaciously broke into the flat when Salvador and his wife Gala were away and systematically made love in every room, often on priceless works of art, although they apparently spared Gala's bed as a mark of respect. During the acrobatics, Gainsbourg kept one eye on the astrakhan on the walls and ceiling, which he later copied. The sunken bath and chandelier in 5 bis were also in imitation of Dalí's bathroom.

Elsewhere we find a table decorated with over 250 pieces relating to law enforcement, including police medals, handcuffs, bullet cartridges and a book opened to pages depicting a Browning revolver. One assumes he took inspiration from Des Esseintes' nautical kitchen with 'the chronometers and compasses, the sextants and dividers, the binoculars and charts scattered about on a side-table which was dominated by a single book'. Towards the end of his life, when his drinking was out of control, Gainsbourg made acquaintance with members of the local con-

TORTOISE
Cold tones of scraped zinc along a hard carapace.
CAT. Home

AQUAMARINE
Sea-green with subdued brilliance.
CAT. Home

stabulary, and would wander down to the police station to chat to gendarmes at 4am because he couldn't find anyone else awake to drink with. Whilst there he would inveigle badges and other law enforcement ephemera from officers, then take them home and add them to his collection.

Another table across the room is decorated with vinyl 45s by forty-five women Gainsbourg wrote chansons for as the *éminence grise* of literate French pop: Brigitte Bardot, Isabelle Adjani, Catherine Deneuve, Françoise Hardy, Nana Mouskouri, Anna Karina and so on. Des Esseintes' recounts a number of sexual adventures in *Against Nature*; Gainsbourg could let photography do the boasting for him, filling the apartment with pictures of beautiful women in various states of undress, most of whom he'd been *in flagrante* with at one time or another. There's a striking, lifesize picture of Bardot, Gainsbourg's paramour prior to Birkin, that would once have greeted visitors as they entered the place.

Gainsbourg may no longer be with us, but his apartment still is, not that you'll be able to see inside this modern day conundrum anytime soon. Plans had been afoot to open it

as a museum, though its bijou dimensions are such that patrons traipsing through would endanger the contents of the former living space. 'With the museum not really happening, I realised I couldn't rent it, I couldn't sell it, I couldn't do anything else with it, so it's been a struggle,' admits Charlotte. 'I think something will happen but I don't think it will happen soon.' For now, Serge Gainsbourg's fans can content themselves with the graffiti on *le mur* Gainsbourg outside the apartment, his plot at Montparnasse Cemetery where fans leave cigarettes, metro tickets and cabbages, and his waxwork of dubious similitude at the Musée Grévin.

JEREMY ALLEN is writing an English language biography of Serge Gainsbourg, to be published next year. He repudiates the label 'Francophile' but will accept 'Parisophile' if pushed (even if it isn't really a word).

NIGHTMARE
by Lydia Davis

I am standing in a very high place from which there is no safe way down. I must get down, but if I begin to descend, I will surely fall to my death. In every version of this recurring dream I am at or near the peak of some sort of natural formation, a rocky summit. On every side, the slope is nearly straight down. There are no footholds or handholds. Sometimes there is a narrow step well below me, but the slope is so steep that if I tried to step down, I would fall outward, into empty space. I read a description recently of a type of stepwell in India that made me experience the same fear as in the dream: the many long steps down to the well are very steep, and slick with damp, mossy growth; there are no handholds.

I had had this dream a number of times when I found myself in a real situation that resembled the dream. My son and I had climbed up to see an old fortress on top of a small Catalonian mountain by the sea. We had ascended an easy slope and explored the fortress. Then I realised that we needed to descend quickly to catch our bus, and I started off down a steeper route, only realising after a few feet that below me, now, was a sheer cliff. I panicked — I thought there was no way back up, either, without sliding on the rubble. It was my son who, standing in a safer spot, calmed me and guided me step by step over to where he was. I wonder now why, having experienced this so often before in a dream, I allowed it to happen in actuality.

REVIEW

A trio of readers, including singer Marc Almond, turn an ambitious novel into an ambitious album. GERT JONKERS evaluates.

TO SING A BOOK

Before we get to poetry, some figures. The English singer Marc Almond OBE has made something like thirty albums (debatable, depending what you call an album, a box set, rerelease, EP, etc.) and has sold over thirty million albums worldwide. That's an average of one million per album. Some

PIANO
Then again, secular music is a promiscuous art in that you cannot enjoy it at home.
CAT. Music

surely have sold more than that, such as his debut with Soft Cell with the number 1 hit 'Tainted Love' on it, or his fabulous duet with Gene Pitney, 'Something's Gotten Hold Of My Heart', from 1989. Naturally, some works sold less. Sometimes deliberately so. Almond's album *Against Nature*, released in 2015 and based on Huysmans' bizarre novel, appeared in a official print run of 125 copies on CD, plus, I need to correct myself here, a few more CDs and vinyl records that the people who pledged the actual making of the album via Kickstarter got as an incentive. Here the calculations become a bit muddy, but I think about 135 people got a (sometimes signed, depending on their generosity)

vinyl album, and maybe 350 Kickstarting fans received the CD. (Some went for the Kickstarter option to have tea at the Wolseley with Almond and his co-authors — I don't know if they got an album too, but I assume so.)

Anyway, this is a rare Marc Almond album. It's not available on Spotify or YouTube. In that sense this piece of text is different from ordinary album reviews: the reader cannot agree or disagree, since there's hardly a way to hear this album and judge for oneself.

There are fifteen songs on *Against Nature*. The first one's called 'Ennui'. The ninth goes by the name of 'My Obsessions'. 'Me and My Coffin', towards the end, has

ILLUSION
'More cunning and contemptible than the impoverished aristocracy and the discredited clergy, the bourgeoisie borrowed their frivolous love of show and their old-world arrogance, which it cheapened through its own lack of taste, and stole their natural defects, which it turned into hypocritical vices.'

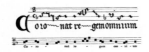

GREGORIAN CHANT
*As massive and imposing as
blocks of freestone.*
CAT. Music

an equally Huysmansian title. Like the book that inspired Almond and his co-writers Jeremy Reed and Othon, it's a hugely dramatic affair, to say the least. Holy fuck! Composer Othon sits behind a grand piano, there's a small string ensemble, and Almond stands behind a big, big microphone, belting his head off! It's also a very 'lyrical' album. Readers are perhaps familiar with that phenomenon of listening to a song for years, singing along even, yet never really understanding the lyrics. Like, I love ELO's 'Don't Bring Me Down', but I've never known what Jeff Lynn sings in the chorus. Don't bring me down, Proust? As in Marcel Proust? Or brousse, the lovely white Corsican cheese? Swoosh, courtesy of Nike? (An online ELO lyrics database claims it's 'groos', whatever that means.) Anyway, that does not happen with a singer like Marc

Almond. He ar-ti-cu-lates. I wonder if this album would better file under 'spoken word', with how he hammers home his words. It's an acquired taste, and a genre that has its fans and enemies, but that's totally gripping at times. Has anybody seen Martin Scorsese's recent Dylan film *Rolling Thunder Revue* and noticed what an amazing version of 'Hurricane' is in it? The tale of a boxer being falsely locked up for murder is being spat out by Dylan and his backing singers with a kind of rhythmic anger that reminds me of community theatre. Subtle? No. (Weirdly, this very version doesn't appear on the film's official soundtrack.)

Against Nature is hugely theatrical and camp, with an emphasis on emphasis, and on the repeat use of quite demanding vocabulary. I WANTED BLACK FLOWERS! I WANTED BLACK FLOWERS! I WANTED BLACK FLOWERS! (In 'Flowers and Cannibals'.) Or Fake! Fake! Fake! She's fake! Fake! Fucking Fake! Fake! etc. (In 'Uranian Blues', which also has a hilarious 'cha-cha-cha-cha' part.) The lyrics (by Jeremy Reed) are obviously based on the novel: the tortoise, the trip to

England, etcetera, but not too literally so. I mean, I do not remember anything about 'bored with backrooms and bars' from the book, or someone 'conducting the rites to my own funeral'. But they could have been in the book, and so Huysmans' 'vibe' is there, on lots of levels. The craziness, the fussiness, the nauseating ketchup of colours. 'True absinthe is blue,' 'bright purple water,' 'myself with green hair,' and, why not, 'the head on a platter, delivered in red sauce'.

'Indigo and oranges I chose for my decor', Almond sings in the sweepingly beautiful chorus of 'Indigo and Oranges', with a melody to die for, preceded and followed by some horrible, stuttering verses. Beauty and horror, just like the book! Very few people will ever hear it.

GERT JONKERS is editor-in-chief of *Fantastic Man* and a founder of *The Happy Reader* and *BUTT* magazine. He spent his first decade in journalism writing about music in the form of album and concert reviews and interviews with the likes Jeff Buckley, Elton John, Daft Punk, 2 Unlimited, Jon Bon Jovi and Cher. He's never met Marc Almond but has seen Soft Cell live in concert, at Paradiso, Amsterdam, on 3 May 2002.

NIGHTMARE
by Seb Emina

I won't name the friend in question. These things are awkward enough in person, let alone in print. But in a recent nightmare I learned of his death via a push alert on my phone. The alert appeared like a 'breaking news' headline but it was just two or three peoples' names plus their ages and causes of death, written in white text over a friendly shade of blue. It had been delivered by an app whose sole purpose seemed to be to send notices of those who'd died of unnatural causes, and to do so almost immediately: it somehow knew before anyone else. My friend's cause of death was 'skiing accident'. Coincidentally, it turned out that I was staying at his parents' chalet. When the news arrived I'd been out for a walk in a beautiful lakeside village. When I returned they were acting normally, so they hadn't heard the news. Before I could work out how to bring up the fact I'd been informed of their son's death via iPhone notification (was this service even trustworthy?) the landline rang. I wondered if it would be the police but it was just a neighbour. I braced myself to say what I had to say.

Images: Shutterstock, Alamy

POLITICS

If we all turn ourselves into works of art, there will be consequences. In light of poet dictators and reality TV presidents, TARA ISABELLA BURTON traces the curious path from dandyism to fascism.

A HARMFUL SOURCE OF FUN

One hundred years ago, an Italian poet conquered a Croatian city. The infuriatingly talented womanising dandy Gabriele D'Annunzio — by then a hero of the First World War, who had famously piloted warplanes over occupied cities in order to airdrop his own propagandistic poetry — marched, with a few of his closest supporters, to the port city of Fiume (now

NIDULARIUM
Sword shaped petals revealing gaping flesh-wounds.
CAT. Flowers & Plants

Rijeka, in Croatia). Formerly Habsburg, largely ethnically Italian, Fiume was — to D'Annunzio — an *unredeemed* city: one a newly national Italy should subsume into itself. But, more importantly, Fiume was a stage: an empty space onto which D'Annunzio could project his ambitions. These ambitions were not purely, or even largely, about political power. Rather, D'Annunzio wanted to create his life, and his world, as a work of art. Under the fifteen months of his *de facto* dictatorship, Fiume was transformed into an ideological carnival — a city of daily poetry readings and nightly firework displays, of occult gatherings and Futurist manifesto-writing — so much

freewheeling free love that syphilis outstripped any other medical complaint by a factor of fifteen. Officially anarcho-syndicalist, implicitly proto-fascist, D'Annunzio's Fiume was the ultimate cult, not just of his highly idiosyncratic personality, but of the cult of personality itself. It was, you might say, the first — and last — truly decadent state.

D'Annunzio's decadence was not purely about sex (though he had a lot of it), nor cocaine (though he had a lot of that, too). Rather, he was interested in unfettering not the appetite but the ego. To be a *dandy* and to be *decadent* converged in one single idea: to create one's identity so fully and so artistically as to leave no scope for the agency, or identity, of another. Although he later became an avowed Italian nationalist, D'Annunzio was very much a child of the French *fin de siècle*.

He was a contemporary of fellow decadent Joris-Karl Huysmans. D'Annunzio's breakout novel, *Il Piacere* (*The Child of Pleasure*), another story of a neurasthenic

CALADIUM
Swollen, hairy stems supporting huge heart-shaped leaves.
CAT. Flowers & Plants

aesthete disillusioned by the vagaries of the modern world, was published in 1889, five years after *Against Nature*. His dandyism was informed by French novelist, fabulist and arch-dandy-theorist Barbey

VALERIAN
Its odour is unpopular with Europeans.
CAT. Flowers & Plants

D'Aurevilly, for whom the true end of the dandy was not sartorial splendour but rather total agency; divinized dandies who double as 'miniature Gods, who always try to create surprise by remaining impassive.'

In the decades after the Fiume experiment — which imploded at Christmas of 1920, as much from internal neglect as from the exasperation of the Italian government — D'Annunzio became better-known as the father of fascism than as the child of decadence. His successors and admirers — most notably Benito Mussolini — modelled their own political projects after his. The aesthetization of politics D'Annunzio pioneered, the utterly *religious* cult of meaning he created around himself — all these reappeared in crueller forms throughout the twentieth century (and, one might argue, well into the Trumpian

CALADIUM ALBANE
As if fashioned out of the
bladder of a pig.
CAT. Flowers & Plants

twenty-first). 'The logical result of Fascism is the introduction of aesthetics into political life,' Walter Benjamin wrote in 1936. When it comes to D'Annunzio, the same was true in reverse. The introduction of aesthetics into public life led inexorably to fascism.

But it's impossible to understand D'Annunzio, or fascism, or the recursive hall-of-mirrors of contemporary post-Trump, post-Kardashian culture — an era in which we are *all* miniature gods, demanding, then fetishizing, our collective *Göttendamerung* — without going back to its source: the alienated 'life-as-art' of Huysmans and *Against Nature*. Dostoevsky famously said that all Russian authors came out of Gogol's overcoat. In 2019, we've all come out from under Des Esseintes' famous pet tortoise.

Against Nature is often remembered — when it is remembered at all — as a decadent novel in the vaguest and most *jejune* sense ('a breviary

of decadence,' Arthur Symons called it). It's about fine furniture and delicious food and anti-clerical imagery and vague moral corruption, with a *pro forma* Christian ending tacked on to the last paragraph to appease the censors. But the novel — a glimpse into the mental collapse of the aristocratic Des Esseintes, who tries and fails to create a cloistered *theïbade raffiné* (a 'refined hermitage') in his family estate in Fontenay, on the outskirts of Paris — is more complex than that. Des Esseintes isn't simply trying to amass beauty, or even grotesque oddities. He's trying to create a new Eden, a world in which he is the only deciding agent. He's trying, in other words, to play God. In the novel's most famous scene, he becomes convinced that the natural colours of a tortoise's shell are so vastly inferior to the artificial ones of gemstones that he decides to encrust his pet tortoise's shell with jewels. The tortoise dies almost

immediately. It's a bizarre re-telling of Genesis: a reference to any one of the dozens of 'world-tortoises' that create the world on their backs. Only, this one is entirely inorganic, purely lapidary. It is a world of total artificiality: one that refuses to engage at all with what we might call the *given* — the world of biological facticity, of necessity, of other people. Of what Heiddegger calls *thrownness*: the world into which we are flung, and in which we cannot help but live.

Time and time again in *Against Nature* Des Esseintes tries to remake the world in his own image. He creates a symphonic 'mouth-organ' in which different liquors are associated with different musical instruments according to a categorisation system based not on allegorical tradition or established myth but rather on his own intuitive sense of what reminds him of what. He tries to give up food altogether to live off peptone enemas. He makes his servants — never named, never given lines — dress like nuns.

Although his aesthetic is a nostalgist's — he's prone to daydreaming about how much better things were in the Me-

BEGONIA
Tuberous.
CAT. Flowers & Plants

dieval era — Des Esseintes is nevertheless a scion of a new, mechanical era. One in which human beings, newly armed with the tools of creation, are delirious at their own possibility. 'Nature has had her day,' he reflects, early in the novel. 'When all is said and done, what a narrow, vulgar affair it all is… not one of her inventions, deemed so subtle and so wonderful, which the ingenuity of mankind cannot create; no Forest of Fontainebleau, no fairest moonlight landscape but can be reproduced by stage scenery illuminated by the

ALOCASIA
Supreme masterpiece of artifice.
CAT. Flowers & Plants

electric light; no waterfall but can be imitated by the proper application of hydraulics, till there is no distinguishing the copy from the original.'

Des Esseintes' anti-modern alienation is inextricable from his thoroughly modern disillusionment with Nature. 'Yes, there is no denying it,' he concludes, '[Nature] is in her dotage and has long ago exhausted the simple-minded admiration of the true artist; the time is undoubtedly come when her productions must be superseded by art.'

There are only two categories for Des Esseintes, we learn: a binary that persists throughout the corpus of decadent and dandyist literature more broadly. There are the autonomous creators, the miniature gods, those who don't just live *their* life as art but transform their surroundings into supporting

ECHINOPSIS
Ghastly pink blossoms.
CAT. Flowers & Plants

players in that illusion. And then there is the crowd, *la foule*: that mass of teeming bodies, evoked in language at once of swarming Nature and of bourgeois mechanical reproducibility. (Des Esseintes describes women, at one point, as 'so many automata wound up at the same time with the same key'). One must be a creator, a dandy, a miniature god, to avoid the indignity of being merely a *creation*: whether of a careless nature or an equally anamic society.

Des Esseintes' obsession with originality, with irreducibility, is a repudiation both of the seeming sameness of Nature and the equally horrific sameness of the era of mechanical reproduction. Nature is cyclical, its bounty repeatable, as is the provenance of the production line, but at Fontenay, every treasure is specific, as irreproducible as Des Esseintes believes himself to be.

The 'Christian' ending of *Against Nature* — Des Esseintes faces his mortality, his biological contingency, his *thrownness*, and prays for the salvation of his soul as he re-enters the created world once more — far from being an abrupt add-on, is baked into the work. *Against Nature* is at once an examination of the appeal of living 'life as art' in an age that seems bereft of any greater meaningfulness, and a clear-eyed condemnation of it. Des Esseintes is a human being, one of the *foule* after all. He must live life as life, too.

Other decadent-dandyist authors of the nineteenth century — Baudelaire, Rodenbach, Villiers de l'Isle-Adam, Lorrain, and, yes, D'Annunzio — all explored and critiqued the problem of self-creation in similar ways. For all of these authors, self-creation is a Miltonian act of defiance: an appropriation of the divine

perspective in the face of a God who appears to be absent or nonexistent altogether. But only for D'Annunzio did the clarion call of 'life as art' manifest itself so clearly off the page. D'Annunzio's Fiume was Des Esseintes' Fontenay made flesh: an entire manufactured city, and culture, that existed only to make D'Annunzio D'Annunzio. Never mind the blood he shed — death and renewal alike were just part of D'Annunzio's fundamental self-narrative: that he was the centre of the world, that the end of both politics and history revolved around *him*. 'I am beyond right and left,' D'Annunzio liked to say, '[as] I am beyond good and evil'.

Ultimately, for D'Annunzio, destruction — his, other people's, that of The World in a grander sense — was exciting.

NEPENTHES
In shape and form passes all the bounds of eccentricity.
CAT. Flowers & Plants

It bolstered his sense of being in a good story. In 1895, he famously proposed a toast at a Venetian dinner party to 'putrefaction' and to the destruction of one world order and the advent of the new. 'I drink,' he exclaimed, 'to the roses which will flower from the blood.'

Today, of course, 'life as art' has been democratised. We do not need to be *Il Vate*, — as D'Anunnzio was often called — nor to conquer a Croatian city, in order to be the miniature gods of our own narratives. The disembodied nature of the Internet has allowed each of us the space to create, unfettered, our own digital Fontenays;

THE ONLY POETS WORTH READING

Strict instructions from the library of Des Esseintes

Name: Ernest Hello
Born: 1828, Brittany
Died: 1885, Brittany
Studied: Law

—

'Extraordinary things can only be stammered out.'

Name: Venerable Bede
Born: c.673
Died: 735, Northumbria
Day job: Monk

—

'I am my own secretary; I dictate, I compose, I copy all myself.'

Name: Léon Bloy
Born: 1846, Dordogne
Died: 1917, Paris
Disliked: Businesspeople

—

'The Eiffel Tower is a truly tragic street lamp.'

Name: Marcus Annaeus Lucanus
Born: 39, Córdoba
Died: 65, Rome
Known as: Lucan

—

'Nobody ever chooses the already unfortunate as objects of his loyal friendship.'

Name: Gregory of Tours
Born: 538, Auvergne
Died: 594, Loire Valley
Day job: Bishop of Tours

—

'A great many things keep happening.'

Name: Tristan Corbière
Born: 1845, Brittany
Died: 1875, Brittany

—

'Come, it's there, in the shade... — A toad!'

Name: Jules Barbey d'Aurevilly
Born: 1808, Normandy
Died: 1889, Paris

—

'I have been as dandy as one can be in France.'

Name: Paul the Deacon
Born: c.720, Lombardy
Died: 799, Latin Valley
Known for: *History of the Lombards*

—

'In comparison with your monastery the palace is a prison.'

Name: Gustave Flaubert
Born: 1821, Normandy
Died: 1880, Normandy

—

'One of the things that proves that art is completely forgotten is the quantity of artists one finds swarming about.'

Name: Petronius
Born: 27, Marseille
Died: 66, Cumae (Naples)
Advisor to: Nero

—

'I said everything that a painful swelling in one's libido tells one to say.'

Name: Émile Zola
Born: 1840, Paris
Died: 1902, Paris
First job: Publicist

—

'What will be the death of me are bouillabaisses, food spiced with pimiento, shellfish, and a load of exquisite rubbish which I eat in disproportionate quantities.'

Name: Apuleius
Born: c.124, Algeria
Died: c.170, unknown
Known for: *The Golden Ass*

—

'A fiend in a fight but not very bright, hot for a crotch, wine-botched, rather die than let a whim pass by — that was her.'

Name: Charles Baudelaire
Born: 1821, Paris
Died: 1867, Paris
Muse: Jeanne Duval

—

'Many a flower casts away / Its sweetly secret fragrance on / The wastes of deepest solitude.'

Name: Aldhelm
Born: c.639, Wessex
Died: 709, Somerset
Known for: His Anglo-Saxon riddles

—

'I share now with the surf one destiny.'

Name: Edmond de Goncourt
Born: 1822, Grand Est
Died: 1896, Paris
Brother: Jules de Goncourt

—

'Never has a virgin, young or old, produced a work of art.'

Name: Boethius
Born: c.477, Rome
Died: 524, Lombardy
Day job: Senator

—

'If you pour wine into the sea the wine is not mingled with the sea but is lost in the sea.'

ANTHURIUM
*An aroid recently imported
from Colombia.*
CAT. Flowers & Plants

indeed, our Fiumes, without infringing on that of others quite so obviously. The implicitly nihilistic idea that our selfhood *demands* total agency, that to be a *creator* is the only way out of our crisis of potential non-being, is now so deeply encoded into our culture that the alternative — pure contingency, terrifying *thrownness* — is unthinkable. *Be your best self* — 'life as art's' more palatably worded contemporary equivalent — is millennial digital culture's *de facto* mantra.

We make our own worlds, our own rules. Seventy-four percent of American millennials now say that they agree with the statement 'whatever is right for your life or works best for you is the only truth you can know.'

The politics of 'life as art' at Fiume have given way, inexorably, to an expanded culture of aesthetic alienation. We watch our own selves, our would-be lovers, our elected leaders, through a glass, darkly: a reality television star has become President, all news

is fake news, and this is both cause for public handwringing and, deeper down, private catharsis. As Constance Grady wrote for *Vox* earlier this year: 'Since 2015, when Donald Trump began his campaign for president in earnest, it has become increasingly common to joke about the news as if it were a TV show. A standard meme now is to say something like, 'Wow, this season of America is really going off the rails. What's going on in that writers' room?' Or, as Walter Benjamin put it, back in 1936: our 'self-alienation has reached such a degree that [we] can experience [our] own destruction as an aesthetic pleasure of the first order.'

We fetishize our narrative arcs, and the tragedy in which they seem poised to end. Our most successful pop stars — Taylor Swift, say, or Lana Del Rey — are those that revel in the artificiality of their emotions: who bring a nihilistic wink to their performance of love, or loss, or death, and whose subtext to every song is *it's all a big joke, anyway.* We're obsessed with Instagram scammers like Caroline Calloway, who (a recent essay in *The Cut* revealed) had her entire heavily aesthetic Instagram feed ghostwritten by her poorer, shyer, best friend.

We are living in the end of history, and it's *sexy.* The natural end of 'life as art' manifests itself in freewheeling

dissociation. Nothing really matters, except that we're in the grip of a compelling story. As Leonard Cohen once wrote: 'I've seen the future, baby, it is murder.'

It is perhaps ironic, and perhaps inevitable, that 'life as art' — once Des Esseintes' one

CYPRIPEDIUM
Oozes drops of viscous paste.
CAT. Flowers & Plants

salvo against the onslaught of reproducibility, his *one claim* to originality — has become, well, a meme. What began as an existential desire to resist being part of *la foule* has become, between the age of D'Annunzio and the age of Trump, an integral part of *la foule* itself.

These days, we are all drinking to the roses that will flower from the blood.

Or, to put it 2019's way: rosé, all day.

TARA ISABELLA BURTON is the author of the novel *Social Creature* and the forthcoming nonfiction *Strange Rites: New Religions for a Godless Age.* She is a contributing editor at *The American Interest* and a columnist at *Religion News Service.*

NIGHTMARE
by Jeanette Winterson

The night is starless. The sky is clear. I have to cross a busy road that seems wide to me. The headlight glare is confusing and the noisy powerful animal-cars don't see me. They are fast and frightening.

But I get across the road.

Now the earth underneath me is cool. The air temperature is chilly. Soon I will need to find a place to sleep where I won't be disturbed. Down here in the woods there is peace and I am not afraid.

I am hungry though. What can I find to eat? Windfall apples, berries. I need to eat before I can sleep. I go on pushing through the leaves. Then I see it, steaming and bright, a bowl filled with something delicious.

ILLUSION
'He wanted a work of art both for what it was in itself and for what it allowed him to bestow on it; he wanted to go along with it and on it, as if supported by a friend or carried by a vehicle, into a sphere where sublimated sensations would arouse within him an unexpected commotion, the causes of which he would strive patiently and even vainly to analyse.'

Who left it there for me?

I go over, crackling the ground, panting a bit. I can't see too well but I can smell everything.

I drink it all, all, all.

And then I know it's not a dream anymore. This is my worst fear. This is true. Already the snow is falling. Soon it will be winter. What shall I do?

This is the dream. This is the nightmare.

I am a hedgehog who drank a pint of coffee and couldn't hibernate.

The emperor Elagabalus is one of *Against Nature*'s relentless parade of name-drops, his debauchery of a piece with Huysmans' lustful atmosphere. NINA MARTYRIS offers an offshore footnote for a cruel but fascinating dictator.

ELAGABALUS

Caligula and Nero are widely regarded as the gold standard of Roman depravity. But they pale in comparison to Elagabalus, the boy-emperor whose reign (218 to 222 CE) was a four-year-long sexual and religious orgy.

A handsome teenager who came to power at the unstable age of fourteen, Elagabalus was guilty of the garden-variety hedonism that is the hallmark of Rome's rulers: eating cockscombs taken from living birds; serving his guests rice mixed with pearls; and demanding meals composed entirely of one colour, blue one day, red the next. His frat-boy malice manifested itself in the false ceiling that he installed in his banqueting hall which, when tipped open, unleashed a deluge of flowers so vast that his guests (who were no doubt busy picking the pearls from their rice) were smothered to death by the perfumed cascade.

But the real reasons for his notoriety are rooted in two intimate aspects of his personality: his sexual orientation and his religious beliefs. Elagabalus, who dressed in women's clothes, had an all-encompassing sexual appetite. And, having been raised as a priest in Syria, one of the first things he did was to replace the reigning Roman deity Jupiter with a black conical stone, the symbol of his sun god. It was hard enough for the Roman establishment to deal with an Eastern ruler who wore fake breasts and makeup without the added outrage of being forced to worship a foreign god.

Like a good teenager with raging hormones, Elagabalus did everything he could to stick it to the old guard, even inducting his mother and grandmother into the senate. The senators were aghast. This was worse than even Caligula's horse. The emperor then decided to marry his sun god to Urania, the moon goddess of Carthage, the

AMBROSIA
Vaporize with lavender and sweet pea for extract of meadow.
CAT. Perfume

sworn enemy of the Romans. Readers will recall that Des Esseintes' American acrobat lover was also called Urania and that he was so deeply stirred by her masculine charms that he felt that there had been a 'change of sex between Urania and himself.' Although Huysmans alludes to Elagabalus by name only once, the emperor's appetites and eccentricities pervade *Against Nature*.

SWEET PEA
A fragrance dominated by orange-blossom.
CAT. Perfume

The litany of Elagabalus' transgressions is dazzling: he visited the brothels dressed as a prostitute; depilated his body, enrobed himself in a cloth of gold encrusted with jewels (like Des Esseintes' doomed turtle), shaved the groins of his male lovers, and had to be stopped from castrating himself. Though his great love was a blond charioteer slave named Hierocles, he married a number of women and, in an unforgivable breach of Roman law, forced himself on a vestal virgin in the vain attempt to have 'godlike children.' He offered to shower wealth on any surgeon who could give him female genitalia. This of course proved impossible. But he consoled himself by calling Hierocles his husband and referring to himself as the wife. Or rather as the battered wife, for he enjoyed being at the receiving end of their sadomasochistic relationship.

The public swimming pool was the emperor's favourite hunting ground. Scouts were dispatched to look for young men who were well hung. These lusty stalwarts were promptly elevated to lofty public posts, resulting in a phallocracy of actors, dancers, cooks and pimps that turned governance into a travesty. All the senators could do was fume on the sidelines. The fuming started at the crack of dawn every

STYRAX
Rub between fingers for a peculiar smell.
CAT. Perfume

morning when they had to show up to watch the emperor sacrifice cattle and sheep to his god and dance around the altar with a cohort of Syrian women, while the entrails of the beasts

ORANGE BLOSSOM
For lilacs and lindentrees combine with tuberose and almond blossom.
CAT. Perfume

were carried away in golden bowls by military prefects. By far the most horrific practice of his reign was the one involving human sacrifice, with one historian claiming that comely young boys were handpicked for death, and their genitals thrown to the lions, snakes and monkeys caged in the temple zoo.

On the plus side, there were no wars during Elagabalus' short reign, and he did repair a number of key buildings. But this did nothing to save him from the wrath of the Praetorian guard. Fed up with his

debaucheries, they beheaded him and his mother, dragged their headless corpses through the streets and dumped them in the Tiber. He was barely dead when the togas rushed to pass a law forever banning women from the senate.

Modern historians have been inclined to be more sympathetic to Elagabalus, arguing that his sexuality and Syrian origins made him a classic victim of othering. But ancient historians were united in their condemnation. Antique sources are notoriously unreliable and prejudiced, but the tales surrounding him are so plentiful that even when taken, as they should be, with a large grain of salt, there is little doubt that Emperor Elagabalus was flagrantly and unashamedly *à rebours*.

NINA MARTYRIS is a freelance journalist based in Knoxville, Tennessee who writes on food, books and tea. She discovered Elagabalus through a circuitous route: Oscar Wilde's *The Picture of Dorian Gray* led her to the mother text, *À Rebours*, which in turn led her to the boy-emperor whose outrageous exploits make Des Essenties seem almost bourgeois. When it comes to decadence, she says, Elagabalus is the gift that keeps on giving.

TUBEROSE
For sweet pea blend with orange blossom, rose and a drop of vanilla.
CAT. Perfume

NIGHTMARE
by Rob Doyle

The night she told me she loved me, I dreamt I was a passenger in an aeroplane that went down far out over the ocean. I swam from the wreckage and reached the shore of a tropical island. Clambering through the jungle, I came to a clearing where dozens of dancers were being directed in an elaborate choreography by a towering figure I knew to be Satan. Irresistibly, and in terror, I was compelled to join the dance, whose end point I understood to be annihilation. On waking, I tried to tell myself that the nightmare was not prophecy; in the years that followed, after I moved to another continent to be with her, I kept trying.

FOOD & DRINK

Finally, the spirits, which are music-related, because that's Des Esseintes' way of having a drink. Drinks writer RICHARD GODWIN embarks on a practical study of the Huysmans method, exploring literally all its possible applications.

LET'S GET HAMMERED

There are few items in Des Esseintes's home quite as covetable as his 'mouth-organ'. The instrument consists of a *fin de siècle* spectrum of spirits and liqueurs, dispensed from barrels into tiny cups at the touch of a button. The organist doesn't play music so much as *taste* it. 'Des Esseintes would drink a drop here, another there, playing internal symphonies to himself, and providing his palate with sensations analogous to those which music dispenses to the ear.'

In one sense, the synaesthetic synthesiser was very

much of its time. Arthur Rimbaud had recently assigned colours to letters in his sonnet 'Voyelles' ('A black, E white, I red, U green, O blue – vowels / One day I shall speak of your strange beginnings'). Claude Debussy would soon discover that modulating from pentatonic G to B major via C sounds *exactly* like swimming into a cathedral. Meanwhile Joris-Karl Huysmans was intuiting that violins are brandy, flutes are crème de menthe, and green Chartreuse is in a major key.

But we should not overlook Huysmans' far-sightedness as a mixologist. We must remember that he was writing before the cocktail had entered the French home. American-style Sherry Cobblers and Mint Juleps had caused a sensation at the *Exposition Universelle* of 1878 in Paris, where they were served in the head of the Statue of Liberty — but it wasn't until 1889 that the first cocktail book appeared in French: *Méthode pour composer soi-même les boissons américaines, anglaises, italiennes etc.* Note how the new drinks were to be 'composed'. *Against Nature* was

published five year before this, in 1884. The idea of mixing spirits and liqueurs to create new harmonies — triads, chords — was highly avant-garde.

ARAK
Peals of thunder.
CAT. Food & Beverage

Not only did Huysmans predict the language of the cocktail, he anticipated its grammar too. The mouth-organ is no capricious assembly but a machine of careful engineering. Let's take the string section:

Violin = old brandy
Viola = rum
Cello = vespetro
Double bass = 'a fine old bitter'

The brandy of the violins is 'choice and heady, biting and

IRISH WHISKEY
An acrid, carbolic bouquet recalling the dentist.
CAT. Food & Beverage

delicate' — presumably some good Cognac? Contrast with the rum of the violas: 'Stronger, heavier and quieter'. Vespetro, if you're wondering, is a sweet

CHARTREUSE
Major.
CAT. Food & Beverage

yellow Italo–French liqueur, usually homemade by steeping saffron, cinnamon, star anise, vanilla, angelica and similar aromatics in alcohol and sweetening with sugar. (Galliano L'Autentico is perhaps the closest commercial equivalent). Huysmans describes its tone as 'poignant, drawn-out, sad and tender'. As for the 'fine old bitter', Huysmans might have had Amer Picon in mind — a popular bitter orange digestif of the time — or more likely, something dark, woody and medicinal, along the lines of Becherovka or Gammel Dansk.

And what a harmonious quartet that is! It's remarkable how close this is to the basic architecture of the original 'cocktail' (spirit + sweetness + bitterness), these days known

GIN
A blare that raises the roof of the mouth.
CAT. Food & Beverage

as an Old Fashioned, but it was brand new when Huysmans was writing. Indeed, Huysmans' combination is precisely the sort of clever Old Fashioned twist I can imagine being served in a hip speakeasy-type bar like Dead Rabbit in New York, 135 years later. It would be called 'The Des Esseintes' and it would be served in a diaphanous crystal tumbler with a large cube of ice and an orange zest twist and a monologue from the barman about this crazy French book he's been reading.

There is a shrewdness to Huysmans' woodwind section, too, comprised of fruit and herbal liqueurs that you wouldn't want to drink too much of on their own, but which are delicate and suggestive in cocktails:

Clarinet = dry curacao
(i.e. orange liqueur)
Oboe = kümmel
(i.e. caraway liqueur)
Flute = crème de menthe
or anisette

It seems a shame to have the flutes represented by *two* liqueurs – but perhaps we could tweak that by assigning anisette (sweet aniseed liqueur) to the piccolos? And while we're at it, we can flesh out the section with a few instrument-alcohols not covered by Huysmans:

Cor anglais = crème de violette
Bassoon = coffee liqueur
Bass clarinet = Grand Marnier

For the brass, Huysmans opts for neat spirits:

Trumpet = kirsch
Cornet = gin
Trombone = whisky
Tuba = marc-brandy (i.e. fairly basic brandy)

I would personally switch gin and kirsch around, but again,

the logic is sound: big clanging spirits for big clanging instruments. Much as the Russian chemist Dmitri Mendeleev had left spaces in his Periodic Table for elements still to be discovered, so Huysmans leaves ample room for:

French horn = pisco
Flugelhorn = aquavit
Euphonium = grappa
Saxophone = tequila

Needless to say, the different age expressions of tequila would correspond to different saxophones: the soprano would

ANISETTE
At once sweet and tart.
CAT. Food & Beverage

be silver tequila, bright and reedy; the tenor sax would be reposado tequila, dusty and lusty; the baritone sax would be añejo tequila, swarthy and brooding — but I fancy smoky, seedy mezcal would take the alto part.

Now that we are tinkering, we might want to rethink Huysmans' percussion section too. He specifies arak (a dry Levantine anise spirit) for cymbals and mastic (a resinous Greek liqueur) for bass drum. But percussion is rum, surely? Rum countries tend to have good rhythm. It even rhymes: 'a rush on rum / of brush and drum' as Laura Nyro sang in 'New York Tendaberry'. And just as there are brooding Jamaican dark rums and good-time Guyanese

ANOTHER WORLD OF INTERIORS
Superabundant decor never quite satisfies: deep down, Des Esseintes craves nothing so much as life in a monk's cell. Photographed by RENÉ BURRI, this chamber is at Le Corbusier's La Tourette, a monastery in the Rhône village of Eveux-sur-Arbresle.

golden rums and spirited Cuban light rums and they all get along famously in a Zombie, well, there are also congas and maracas and hi-hats and tambourines and the more of them being bashed at once, the better. So I say we reassign the viola rum part to, say, calvados. And reassign:

Percussion = rum(s)

And since rum is made from sugar and sugar is in *itself* a key cocktail ingredient, I would add (bear with me):

Drum kit = sugar syrup

And now we are in the twentieth century. Oh, well?

Acoustic guitar = Irish whiskey
Electric guitar = Bourbon
Distorted electric guitar = Rye
Bass guitar = Angostura bitters
Fender Rhodes = Campari
Hammond organ = Aperol

The geographical specialities should be self-explanatory:

Banjo = corn whiskey
Pedal steel = Southern Comfort
Accordion = absinthe
Bouzouki = ouzo
Hawaiian guitar = okolehao
Javanese bonang = arrack

However:

Bagpipes = baiju

As for electronic instruments, I'm pretty sure that:

Synthesiser = vodka

And also that:

'80s production = Midori
'90s production = Baileys
'00s production = Jägermeister
'10s production = Fernet-Branca

Which leaves the quandary of the piano. It would have to

be something rich and versatile that satisfies all on its own. Wine? Not a liqueur, you protest! Well, it's true, you wouldn't waste an 1882 Chateau Lafite Rothschild on a cocktail (the 1883 on the other hand…). But champagne *is* a frequently used cocktail

RUM
Strong, heavy and quiet.
CAT. Food & Beverage

ingredient. And consider all the spiced and fortified wines that ushered in the golden age of the cocktail: upright French vermouths; honky-tonk Italian vermouths; jazzy quinquinas like Byrrh and Dubonnet; Lillet Blanc, the Steinway of aperitifs; Carpano Antica Formula, the Bösendorfer of the back-bar…? And this is before we have considered all the ports and sherries! I suppose you might need a dozen or so tiny cups to capture all of the necessary tones. But yes, the more I think about it the more:

Piano = wine(s)

Still, before we add any more embellishments to Des Esseintes's instrument, we should appreciate its original subtleties. Huysmans wouldn't be so basic as to have a unidimensional instrument. 'The music of liqueurs had its own scheme of interrelated tones,' he notes, before supplying the mind-blowing information that

VESPETRO
Poignant, drawn-out, sad and tender.
CAT. Food & Beverage

green Chartreuse corresponds to the major scale and Bénédictine to the minor. Des Esseintes plays crème de cassis to suggest the song of a nightingale, and cacaochouva (an old-fashioned chocolate liqueur) to summon a pastoral lullaby. Clearly, there is a whole painting-box of sonorities to be evoked by crème de peche, Cherry Heering, blue curacao, Pisang Ambon, pear eau-de-vie, etc — to say nothing of the tonalities of lemons, limes, cream, eggs, mint, etc.

Occasionally, an original Huysmans mouth-organ, complete with sandalwood barrels, brass spigots and vintage nineteenth-century spirits will pass through Sotheby's or Christies. But the prices are usually prohibitive. Happily, it's not too hard to rig up a rudimentary homemade version with a few shot glasses and egg-cups. If you have a decent

CRÈME DE MENTHE
Soft yet shrill.
CAT. Food & Beverage

booze collection, you might even build up to, say, Gustav Mahler's Ninth Symphony in the key of lemon-Chartreuse. There's something lovely about the way the Galliano heartbeat gives way to muted pisco in the first movement — and the Kahlua-anisette blast at the end of the second movement is inspired. Still, the breakdown of tonality in the fourth movement is not to be attempted lightly. Maurice Ravel's Piano Concerto in raspberry-Chartreuse is perhaps more rewarding for the novice, and the Noilly Prat

KIRSCH
A wild trumpet blast.
CAT. Food & Beverage

theme returning as violette in the second movement is particularly charming.

If your tastes are more contemporary and your alcohol budget more modest, you can replicate Nirvana's *Nevermind*

with little more than a rye whiskey, sugar syrup and bitters, i.e. a punchy sort of Old Fashioned. Fela Kuti's *Expensive Shit* is a riot of rum and tequila; Kraftwerk's *The Man-Machine* iced vodka with a few pipettes of flavoured-schnapps. Miles Davis's *In a Silent Way* still tastes wonderfully avant-garde — a mournful gin solo over layered washes of Campari and Aperol — but I most enjoyed drinking the entirety of Joanna Newsom's second album *Ys*. Huysmans specifies that the harp is 'dry cumin', a little love-it-or-hate it, but the brandy of the strings mellows it out.

If you have a few musicians lying around, it is equally possible to reverse-engineer cocktails into sound. As we've seen, the Old Fashioned (whiskey + sugar + bitters) is guitar, bass and drums. The dry Martini (gin + vermouth) is a trumpet accompanied by a piano. The Stinger (brandy + crème de menthe) is violin and flute. The Bijou, a very Huysmanian combination (gin + sweet vermouth + green Chartreuse + bitters) is trumpet, piano and bass playing in a major key.

There are some gems to be found among the modern classics too. The Conference, a favourite at New York's Death & Co (rye + bourbon + calvados + cognac + bitters) is a Velvet Underground-y two guitars,

viola, violin and bass. The Fernando (bianco vermouth + Fernet-Branca + Galliano) is a piano-cello duet with bang-up-to-date production.

MASTIC
Bangs and beats with all its might.
CAT. Food & Beverage

'The poet becomes a seer by a long, prodigious and rational disordering of all the senses,' Rimbaud wrote in 1871. After all these years, there is still no more reliable way to do that than by listening to music, drinking alcohol, or preferably both. Gin green, ice white, rum blues, jazz red, peach sad. One day we will learn of your strange affinities.

RICHARD GODWIN is a journalist, author of *The Spirits: A Guide to Modern Cocktailing* and inveterate inventor of cocktails, such as the Mexican Jumping Bean: 50ml tequila reposado, 1 shot espresso, 10ml agave syrup, shake over ice and fine-strain into a coupe.

NIGHTMARE
by Yelena Moskovich

We're at the synagogue and I feel tiny. There are way too many round tables. My agent is behind me and she says, You're on next! I rush to the bathroom, because I haven't prepared anything. The door is locked and I hear my brother say, Don't come in! He's doing vocal exercises because he has to sing a harmony with the rabbi. His voice doesn't sound too bad at first. But then it gets fuzzy. The door opens and I come in without a sound. He isn't singing. He's shaving his beard. The electric razor is clipping Hebrew-like words from his dark facial hair. He turns my way and begins swatting at me with a huge hand. I begin yelping, it's me, it's me! But my voice is a pinched, buzzing thing. Damn, I realise I'm a house fly. The rabbi should be here any minute.

POSTCARD

Self-portrait of **ROBERT DE MONTESQUIOU** (1855–1921), Count of the noble Montesquiou-Fézensac family. The poet and aesthete found notoriety when it became clear he'd inspired the character of Jean des Esseintes. Montesquiou really did have an ornamental tortoise (it was painted gold) and a room furnished to resemble a monk's cell.

LETTERS

The inversion of luxury as a lifelong pursuit.

Dear Happy Reader,

I was really delighted to be prompted to re-read *Against Nature*. In the 1990s I applied for a fashion design job that I was unqualified for and had to submit a project that defined 'understated luxury'.

I used the following passage to anchor the design work: 'He decided, in fact, to reverse the optical illusion of the stage, where cheap finery plays the part of rich and costly fabrics; to achieve precisely the opposite effect, by using magnificent materials to give the impression of old rags; in short, to fit up a Trappist's cell that would like the genuine article but would of course be nothing of the sort.'

My years of lounging around reading instead of studying were finally validated and I got the job!

I've built my career on inverting the symbols of luxury and remain indebted to M. Huysmans and M. Des Esseintes.

I'm sure I'm not alone in this anecdote Thanks for the reminder to re-visit.

Leonie Branston
London

Hi Seb,

There's a tiny detail in the last issue of *THR* (a footnote on page 16) that talks about the children's author Matt Christopher. It says that after his death, his family registered his name and was able to publish further eighty books with the help of various ghost-writers. I'm an editor myself, and I'm excited to let you know this has given me the perfect clue for a book we were thinking about, a book about ghostwriting, so now I've found the perfect author to start doing research for the book. That's exactly what we were looking for, so thanks a lot for that.

Jacobo Zanella
Querétaro, Mexico

Hello,

Strange question – but I'm wondering if it's at all possible to find out who makes this blue sweater Owen Wilson is wearing on the cover and throughout the latest issue?

I really like it!

Tristan Eden
New York

The Happy Reader replies: Hmm, it is a nice sweater. We'll do our best to track down the label.

Dear Sir —

Owen Wilson and Amanda Fortini's assessment of Elvis's late, Las Vegas period (*THR13*) warrants a rebuttal. Firstly, 'Suspicious Minds' is majestic. That it should be used as shorthand for Elvis's decline is flagrant. Secondly, the brilliance of Elvis's Las Vegas period lies in the transformation of the juvenile, transgressive energy of 'Hound Dog' into a fully-formed, tour de force live spectacular. Every note, strut, groove and shake is infused with the flair and finesse of two decades as American's greatest performer. I would refer Wilson and Fortini to Jon Landau's epic critique of Elvis's late period in Rolling Stone, Nov. 1971, in which he summarises that, "He is the one and only performer who can simply revel in it [fame and greatness] and us with him."

Regards,
Lee Court
London

Please send commentary, clarifications and anything else you'd like to see published on this page to letters@thehappyreader.com or The Happy Reader, Penguin Books, 80 Strand, London WC2 0RL.

Every society has its old ghost stories: the next Book of the Season is an anthology of tales from Japan, as recorded by an improbable master.

WHICH BOOK NEXT?

The Book of the Season for summer 2020 is *Japanese Ghost Stories*: oral folktales set down as short stories by the nineteenth-century wanderer Lafcadio Hearn.

The stories are fascinating. Time dilates, reality blurs and worlds of life and death collide in mind-bending ways. A cast of phantoms and ghouls lope through the pages, headless or faceless, powerful or just weird. In Hearn's retellings the author himself often appears in their midst, offering commentary and tangential digressions in a self-referential style sometimes described as 'metafolk'.

An itinerant figure with an extraordinary life story packed with more drama than anyone could bear, Hearn was born on a Greek island and then lived in Dublin, London, Cincinnati and New Orleans. When he was thirty-nine he went to Japan as a newspaper correspondent, and ended up staying for the rest of his life. He became a Japanese citizen and married the daughter of a samurai family, with whom he had four children. His Japanese name is Koizumi Yakumo.

To stay on track, read *Japanese Ghost Stories* before the next issue of *The Happy Reader* is published in June 2020. Tell the world what you think the old-fashioned way: by sending an email for publication, addressed as ever to letters@thehappyreader.com.

SUBSCRIBE
The Happy Reader is the world's magazine-shaped book club. Subscribe and never miss an issue by visiting boutiquemags.com

Japanese Ghost Stories is available from bookshops or penguin.co.uk